Eternally Claimed

A PARANORMAL F/F/M VAMPIRE MENAGE ROMANCE

EVERMORE ETERNALS
BOOK TWO

LUNA LAWSON

Lyra

A marvel.

Even to my weary eyes that had seen it all countless times over the last century, I couldn't ignore the shiver that crept up my spine every time I entered Evermore's great fortress. The grand structure loomed over the sprawling city below the high crags, its dark stone walls adorned with intricate carvings of battles won and lost, legends of old, and the creatures of the night who had come before us.

My family home was nowhere near the grandeur of these stone corridors, and I'd been fortunate to have been chosen for the position I did hold. My mother was unwilling to tell me just how she'd been able to secure it for me—and I didn't want to ask.

My mother's ambitions had been poured into my ears for as long as I could remember, and she saw my position as a lady in waiting as a means to an end.

A stepping stone.

A soft breeze brushed past me, carrying with it the scent of the dark roses and nightshade that grew outside the walls of the fortress. It was a heady combination that never failed to remind me of my place within these walls.

The chandeliers above cast flickering shadows on the floor and their candles cast an eerie glow over the gathering darkness outside. I shivered slightly, wrapping my arms around myself to ward off the chill that clung to the air like a lover's embrace.

We were preparing for a grand event, one that would shape the future of our kingdom. A high-profile betrothal announcement between two powerful families was to take place that night, and I had been tasked with ensuring everything was perfect. The decorations needed to be exquisite, a reflection of the union we were about to celebrate.

I busied myself with arranging blood-red roses in ornate vases. Their velvety petals caressed my fingers as I worked and I tried to focus my thoughts on my efforts and forget my mother's incessant scheming.

Dark silk banners emblazoned with the crests of the two families that would be united by this betrothal hung proudly from the rafters, their edges trimmed with delicate silver embroidery.

Long tables had been draped in fine white linen, the settings immaculate and precise, each gleaming silver fork and knife aligned with military precision. Crystal goblets awaited the finest blood-tinged wine to be poured, their delicate facets caught the candlelight and cast it around the room like liquid jewels.

As I worked, I couldn't help but imagine myself as the bride-to-be, standing before the gathered crowd in a gown of silk and lace, a tiara glinting in my dark hair. The thought sent a thrill down my spine, a momentary escape from the reality of my station. But deep down, I knew that such dreams were best forgotten.

I was not alone in the banquet hall, and the noise of conversation from the other ladies filled the air and helped to put me more at ease as I listened to their conversations instead of the flurry of thoughts that tumbled in my mind.

The heavy doors to the banquet hall creaked open, and as if on cue, my heart stuttered in my chest. A tall, imposing figure strode into the room, his broad shoulders filled the doorway with his dark, powerful presence.

General Thorne Valerius.

The Valerius family crest hung on the banner above my head and was emblazoned on the fine place cards that had been set upon the table. The groom to be.

"Make way!" someone called out. I scrambled to stand with the rest of the servants as the general strode into the room. My cheeks burned with embarrassment at having been caught daydreaming.

As he walked past, I couldn't help but notice the sharp angles of his chiseled jawline, the intensity of his dark eyes that seemed to hold secrets within their depths. He carried himself with an air of confidence and authority, his every movement fluid and graceful. I shivered involuntarily, acutely aware of the power that radiated from him—it was intoxicating, irresistible.

I'd be lying if I said that I hadn't imagined what it would be like to be his lover...

"You there," he addressed me, his voice deep and commanding, sending shivers down my spine once more. "What is your name?"

"Me?" I choked out.

I looked up into the general's dark eyes and a shiver rippled down my spine.

"Lyra— Batherst."

"Lyra," he repeated. His lips curved into a smile as though he could hear my darkest, most scandalous, thoughts.

I swallowed hard. My name had never sounded so alluring before. "I trust the preparations are going well?"

"Y-yes, General," I stammered, cursing my lack of composure. "We're almost finished."

"Very good," he replied, his gaze lingering on me for a moment before he continued across the room.

Desire curled in my belly like a living thing, awakening a hunger I had never known. I longed to be close to him, to feel his strong arms around me, to feel the ache of his teeth as they plunged into my skin. It was madness, of course, but I couldn't deny the allure.

I wanted him.

Gods above, what is happening to me?

I couldn't take my eyes off him as he moved through the room and examined the preparations for the evening's event.

My breath caught in my throat as he turned to look in my direction, a knowing smile playing on his lips. I quickly busied myself with adjusting the table settings, trying desperately to ignore the heat that blossomed on my cheeks.

But even as I sternly reminded myself of the consequences, I knew it was too late. The fire General Thorne Valerius had ignited within me could not be so easily extinguished. He was untouchable, but the promise of danger only served to fan the flames of my desire higher and higher, until I feared I might be consumed by them entirely.

"Can you believe the General is *finally* taking a wife?" A girl named Lisette sighed as we both worked on arranging the flowers on the tables. "You never want to see such fine specimens taken off the table, even if you were never going to be able to eat it..."

I bit down on my lip to keep from smiling, but Lisette's eyes glittered with mirth as she nudged me.

"Come on, Lyra. You can't tell me you've never thought about him."

"I— No. Of course not."

Lisette snorted. "Well, you'd be the only one in Evermore who hasn't had filthy thoughts about him." Lisette's eyes were bright and her voice was breathless as she spoke about him, and I felt a flash of jealousy as I glanced in the general's direction.

I bit my lip as I struggled to keep my composure. The mere mention of his name caused a shiver to run down my spine, and my heart raced like a caged bird desperate for escape. His reputation as a vicious fighter and a powerful lover only fueled my desire for him, and I found myself wondering for the hundredth time what it would be like to share his bed, to feel the strength and power of his body entwined with mine.

"He's the youngest general in Evermore's history," Lisette continued. "They say he's nearly unstoppable in battle. It's a shame he's going to be married to that stuck up Palimenteri woman."

"Kristabella Palimenteri?" I blurted out, jealousy flaring within me like a wildfire. I hadn't recognized the other family crest on the banners overhead, and I felt like a fool as the realization dawned on me.

Lisette made a face. "Their betrothal was announced not long ago. My father says that they'll make a powerful couple. Her family is one of the most influential in the kingdom." She cast a sidelong glance at me, her eyes narrowing slightly. "Didn't you know?"

"I'd forgotten," I lied quickly, feeling a blush creep across my cheeks. I turned my attention back to the flowers, pretending to be engrossed in their arrangement. But as I continued to work, I couldn't shake the image of Kristabella—of course I knew who she was. She was beautiful, poised, and so perfectly suited for General Thorne that it made me hate her all the more. It was irrational, but it was an all-consuming hatred born of envy.

"I won't forget," Lisette said grumpily. "I've never been more jealous of anyone in at least a century."

I didn't say anything, but Lisette caught me looking at the general.

"You can pretend you're not jealous all you like," she hissed. "I know what you're thinking."

"You don't know anything," I snapped. I set down another vase and walked away from the table, leaving Lisette to finish her work alone.

I knew I couldn't have him, but there was something about the general that made my heart race, a feeling I could only describe as a mixture of lust and admiration. He was everything I'd ever wanted —powerful, respected, and undeniably attractive.

"Stop it, Lyra," I whispered as I forced my gaze back to the elaborate decorations I was tasked to arrange.

And yet, even as I tried to suppress my desires, I found myself imagining what it would be like to be by his side—not just as a lover, but as an equal, sharing in his power and influence.

Impossible dreams.

Stupid desires.

The scent of candles mixed with the intoxicating aroma of the flowers, created an atmosphere that was both romantic and dangerous—much like the man who continued to occupy my thoughts.

The woman who was supervising our work clapped her hands to call our attention. "Ladies, it is time to finish these preparations. Finish your tasks and return to your posts."

My work was finished, and I didn't want to wait for Lisette to catch up with me. I couldn't listen to her talk about the betrothal celebration, or anything to do with what was happening in the fortress that night. I had entirely too much to think about already.

~

I would only have a few hours of solace until I was expected back at the fortress for the celebration. I would pour wine, clear dishes, and try my best not to make eye contact with my betters...

I tried to close the door silently when I entered the house. But my mother was always listening, and she was waiting for me at the bottom of the stairs, blocking my path to my bedchamber.

"General Thorne is quite a catch, isn't he?" my mother said casually. "Kristabella Palimenteri is a lucky woman. And her father will benefit from this alliance..."

"Indeed," I agreed, bitterness lacing my voice. I turned away from her, intent on finding somewhere I could take a breath and clean my head... the garden—

"Come here," my mother snapped.

I froze in place and turned back toward her.

"Lyra—"

Her tone held a warning and I walked over to her slowly. I stood still as a stone as she brushed her cold fingers over my cheek. "It's a pity your father left us with nothing," she said. "You are far too pretty to be so disadvantaged." She gripped my chin hard and stared into my eyes. "Nothing is set in stone, daughter. Things change, alliances shift—"

I turned my face away from her. "I know," I muttered.

"You know nothing of this world," my mother hissed. "This betrothal could change everything—"

The very mention of General Thorne Valerius and his betrothal to Kristabella Palimenteri gnawed at my heart.

"How?"

"*Darling,* you must see the opportunity this presents," my mother's voice dripped with condescension and her dark eyes gleamed in the candlelight. "With your position as a lady-in-waiting, you have access to the inner circles of society. If you could find a way to get closer to the General, perhaps even secure his... favors, it could greatly benefit our family's standing."

I clenched my fists at my side, feeling both repulsed and intrigued by the idea. To become the General's mistress would be a scandalous affair, yet the temptation to be close to him, to feel his strong hands on my flesh, was undeniable.

"I— Do you truly believe it's worth the risk?" I asked, my voice trembling slightly with uncertainty.

"How could it not be," she replied without hesitation. "You are beautiful enough to captivate even the most stoic of men. At least your father was good enough to provide you with that if he could give us nothing else. You must use your assets to our advantage, Lyra."

As much as I hated to admit it, her words held truth. With a deep breath, I steeled myself for the path that lay ahead. If pursuing the General meant elevating my family's social standing, then I would do what was necessary, regardless of the consequences. And perhaps, in the process, I could satisfy the burning desire that consumed me every time I laid eyes on him.

"Think of the connections, Lyra," my mother said. She stepped down off the stairs and paced the floor in front of them, still blocking my escape.

I watched her intently, her every word stoking the flames of jealousy that raged within me. How could she know that I longed to be the one standing beside General Thorne Valerius, sharing his power and commanding the respect of all who beheld us.

"General Valerius is a highly respected and influential man, Lyra," my mother continued, her voice smooth and measured. "His favor could grant our family opportunities we never dared dream of. Our coffers would overflow, our social standing would soar, and you, my dear, would be at the very heart of it all."

My heart pounded at the thought, my desire for the General intensifying. "Mother, what if... what if there were another way?"

My mother's dark gaze met mine, and I saw a flicker of understanding in their depths. She knew exactly what I was suggesting, and though the idea was scandalous, she did not immediately dismiss it.

"Securing the General's favor directly?" she mused, weighing the possibilities. "Though it might seem unorthodox... if you were to become his mistress, we could still reap the rewards of his influence. He's a powerful man, Lyra, and men like him have secrets. Secrets that, if discovered, could be used to our advantage."

"Blackmail," I whispered, both horrified and intrigued by the notion.

"Only if necessary," she said primly. "But first, you must win his affections. Prove yourself irresistible to him. And then, my dear, we shall have the world at our feet."

My body trembled, torn between repulsion and a desperate longing for the General's touch. It was a dangerous game we were considering—one that could lead to ruin or riches. Yet as I looked into my mother's eyes, I knew that I would do anything, risk everything, for the sake of my family's future.

"Say you will do it," she said.

I nodded. "I will. I will capture his heart."

"His heart is not required," my mother said as her lips curved into a wicked smile. "Now, let us begin plotting your seduction, Lyra. The General won't know what hit him."

As we discussed the sordid details of my plan, dark excitement coursed through me, mingling with the ever-present jealousy that haunted my every waking moment. I would have the General, one way or another, and when I did, his betrothal to Kristabella Palimenteri would mean nothing.

Two

I stood outside the banquet hall and tried to regain control over my desperately pounding heart. I thought I would be ready... but now that I was standing outside the banquet hall, all of my bravado had faded in an instant.

My mother's words spun in my mind.

"You must draw him in with your natural allure. Catch his eye whenever possible, hold his gaze just a moment longer than necessary. Allow your fingers to graze his when passing him a drink, or let your body brush against his in a crowded room."

"Engage him in conversation. Discover his interests and passions, and find common ground. Men like the General crave intellectual stimulation as much as physical pleasure. Show him that you are more than just a pretty face – that you have a mind as sharp as any blade."

"Be bold in your pursuit. While discretion is important, there is something undeniably arousing about forbidden love. Let him know, without doubt, that you want him—perhaps even need him. Whisper heated promises into his ear when you serve his dinner..."

It had all seemed so simple. But now that I was faced with it—I didn't know if I could go through with it. Couldn't there be another way? One that didn't involve being so... obvious?

But how—

My goal was not only to secure his favor but to break the bond between him and Kristabella. To make him want me so intensely that he would forsake all others.

It was a feverish fantasy of seduction and conquest.

The prospect of claiming the General as my own, of reducing him to a helpless captive of my desires, was intoxicating. And yet, beneath the heady rush of power, an undercurrent of fear and doubt still lingered.

If I failed... it would not just be me who burned.

My mother would be punished as well.

But if I succeeded—everything I had always wanted would be mine.

"Lyra—there you are! Lady Hargate is calling for us. Are you ready?"

Lisette.

I forced a smile onto my face. "I'm sorry, I didn't hear—"

"Hurry up," Lisette groaned. She grabbed hold of my hand and pulled me through the stone corridor. "They're all in the gardens— we're supposed to be serving wine."

"Of course," I murmured.

As we entered the gardens, my eyes immediately sought out General Thorne Valerius. He was there among the nobles, his dark hair pulled back neatly into a braid that hung down his back, his broad shoulders and muscular form filled out his formal uniform in a way that made my breath catch.

I couldn't help but feel a sudden wave of desire, the heat pooling low in my belly at the sight of him.

"There she is," Lisette hissed. "Kristabella Palimenteri, herself. Try not to stare, Lady Hargate will have harsh words for us if anyone complains."

My heart clenched at the mention of her name, and I did try not to stare, but it was almost impossible to tear my eyes away. Kristabella was grace personified, with a heart-shaped face framed by black curls and intelligent gray eyes that seemed to hold infinite warmth and kindness. I despised her, not for who she was, but for what she represented —the one obstacle standing between me and the object of my desire.

"She's impossibly beautiful," Lisette sighed. "It's all very unfair. Rich, powerful, and beautiful... no one should have that much luck."

Kristabella was standing near the general, but her gaze wasn't on him. She surveyed the garden with what I could only guess was a critical eye—was she looking for someone? Or simply weighing the value of the nobles in attendance. Whatever it was, she didn't seem to be paying any attention to the general at all. How could she ignore someone like him? All at once, Kristabella turned to him and laid a hand on his arm. My heart sank with bitter jealousy as I watched them, wondering how I could ever hope to compete with such a woman.

And yet... something in me refused to give up so easily.

I took a deep breath and rallied my courage. If I was going to do this, if I was going to make the General mine, I had to start tonight.

I grabbed hold of one of the bottles of wine that Lisette carried and made my way through the crowd toward them, determined to engage him in conversation just as my mother had instructed.

"Good evening," I said as I approached. "May I refill your wine?"

Kristabella's gaze turned to me and she smiled, her full lips tilted in an alluring curve that made my breath catch.

"Very kind of you," she murmured as she held out her goblet toward me.

I swallowed hard as I poured the wine, and I tried not to glance up at the general. I could feel his eyes on me, but I had to focus on keeping my hands from shaking.

"I haven't seen you here before," Kristabella said softly. "What is your name?"

"Lyra Batherst," I replied as I stepped back. "I have— I have only just taken a position in the fortress."

Kristabella's chin tilted. "Batherst, I don't know that name."

"I wouldn't expect you to," I said quickly. "I'm— we're not important."

Her pale gaze swept over me, and I tried not to shiver. "I don't know about that," she murmured. "I hope I will see more of you, Lyra."

Suddenly something occurred to me.

There was another way that I could get close to General Valerius without being discovered.

"I hope so, too," I replied.

I walked back to where Lisette waited for me at the edge of the garden. "What was that," Lisette hissed.

"What?"

She stared at me with wide eyes. "Talking to Kristabella Palimenteri—you know that's not allowed. You're lucky that Lady Hargate didn't see you!"

"You worry too much," I muttered.

"That's how I stay out of trouble," Lisette snapped. "Next you'll be talking to the Queen Mother about her dogs..."

I bit my lip to keep from laughing, but Lisette wasn't wrong. I had to be careful. But I had to find a way to get closer to Kristabella.

The General was out of my reach... but her?

That would be much easier.

At least I hoped it would be.

~

I spent the following weeks dodging my mother's questions about the General, while I meticulously observed Kristabella's habits and acquaintances and tried to calculate the best ways to infiltrate her life.

The key was to get closer to her without arousing suspicion, and that meant I had to become indispensable.

We shared a few passing conversations, while I went about my duties in the fortress and I was thrilled when it seemed that she was searching me out to speak to me about something, no matter how small.

It was working.

"Lyra, would you care to join me for a stroll in the gardens?" she asked one evening.

"I— I'm not finished with my duties—"

"Lady Hargate won't mind," Kristabella said with a conspiratorial smile. "I would like some company."

"Of course, my lady," I murmured. I couldn't deny the triumphant surge in my chest. This was my chance—our first step toward an intimate friendship. As we walked, I kept the conversation light, asking her about her favorite pastimes and carefully listening to every word she said.

"Tell me, Lyra," Kristabella said suddenly as we passed the rose garden and turned down another path that led toward the stone ancient fountains, "what do you think of General Thorne?"

"The General," I choked out. "I— I do not—"

"Come now, you must have some opinion of him. I know that all the servants talk about him. You can't pretend that you haven't heard the gossip."

"Gossip—"

Kristabella sighed and pushed her hard hair over her shoulder. "Come now, Lyra. You can trust me."

My mind raced—*what could I say about him that would not*

give away how I really felt? "Well, he is very... dashing. The other ladies are very fond of discussing him..."

"I'm sure they are," Kristabella murmured with a smile.

"But they all agree that you are very lucky— Several are quite jealous of you."

Her gray eyes flashed as she looked at me. "And you? Are you jealous?"

"I—"

She grabbed hold of my hand and squeezed it gently. "I am teasing you, Lyra," she said. "But you cannot deny that the General has a certain... allure."

"Indeed, he does," I agreed, even as my mind seethed with jealousy and ambition.

I kept these conversations going, always careful to maintain an air of innocence. All the while, my secret desire festered within me —how could I remove Kristabella from the equation and claim General Thorne for myself? I would stop at nothing to achieve my goal.

"My lady, do you ever worry that the General's affections might wander?"

Kristabella laughed and then stopped walking, pulling me to a stop. "I do worry," she admitted. "If the General decided to end this betrothal, it would be the ruin of centuries of planning. My father has been working tirelessly to secure these allegiances..." She shook her head and rubbed her fingers over her collarbone. "General Valerius is surrounded by temptation, and I know there are many who covet his attention, and my position."

"Then allow me to be your eyes and ears, my friend," I offered, placing a comforting hand on her arm. "I might only be a servant, but I see and hear things that others do not. I will watch over him and ensure that he remains true to you."

Kristabella gazed into my eyes as she considered my offer, and then she nodded, a faint smile tugging at her full lips.

"Thank you, Lyra," she replied. "This... loyalty means more to me than you know."

She could never know that my offer was not born of friendship, but of a burning ambition that threatened to consume me. As we continued to walk, our fingers entwined in a gesture of affection, I knew that our growing bond was built on a foundation of deceit. And yet, I felt no remorse—only a fierce determination to see my plan through to the end.

After that night, Kristabella sought out my company more often, and Lady Hargate seemed to turn a blind eye to the fact that I did not complete my duties. I knew that it was Kristabella's influence that guaranteed this, and I was grateful for it. Lisette's questions were too much to bear, and I finally had something to tell my mother when she demanded to know how my plans were progressing.

"We're going into the city," Kristabella said one evening as she pulled me away from my mopping.

"The city?" My heart sank, I dreaded the moment she would ask me to show her my family home—or, my greatest fear, that she would ask to meet my mother. I couldn't bear the thought of my mother speaking to Kristabella, or what would happen afterward.

"I never get to leave the fortress," she said, "but if I have you with me, I know I won't get lost. You'll show me where to go. I've been hearing about the markets and flower sellers for far too long, and I want to see them for myself."

No matter how worried I was about getting in trouble, I couldn't refuse her request.

"I know just the ones," I said as I forced myself to smile. "The night-blooming flowers are always so beautiful at this time of year."

Kristabella's pale eyes were bright as she wound her arm through mine and pulled me along the stone corridors toward the fortress' main gate.

I walked these paths every night, but for some reason, with Kristabella at my side, everything was different.

The guards at the gate who usually didn't bother to even glance in my direction snapped to attention when Kristabella and I passed. She clutched my arm tighter and winked at them and I fought the urge to laugh.

"Don't you ever flirt with the guards?" she whispered.

"Never," I hissed back.

Kristabella laughed and I couldn't help but join in. I worried that someone would stop us, but none of the guards questioned us, and we walked through the fortress gates without hesitation.

For some reason, with Kristabella at my side, I felt braver.

Bolder.

Kristabella and I walked together along the bustling streets of the city, deep in conversation.

"Sometimes, I feel suffocated by the expectations placed upon me," Kristabella confided, her intelligent gray eyes clouded with frustration. "You must feel so... free."

"Free?" I scoffed. "I was scrubbing the fortress floors when you pulled me away from my duties. That's not freedom—"

Kristabella sighed. "But you could marry whoever you wished," she insisted. "No one would tell you who to love—"

My lip curled, but I forced myself to smile instead. "I haven't thought about it."

"I hadn't either—" she said softly.

Inwardly my jealousy simmered. She didn't appreciate all the freedom she had. The freedom that her wealth and position granted her. It was this very freedom that I craved for myself— If I had her life, I would have the freedom to claim General Thorne as my own.

"Oh! The flowers!"

Kristabella released her grip on my arm and rushed toward the flower stalls that marked the edge of the markets. I followed at a dutiful distance and did my best to answer her questions about the decadent blooms.

"You know so much about all of these," she said in a voice filled with awe as she pulled some of the dark flowers to her nose and inhaled their thick scent.

"You should order some for your wedding," I said in what I hoped was a light tone.

Kristabella's nose wrinkled as she set the flowers down and thanked the vendor. "I don't have any say in the flowers. Or my dress. Or... anything, really," she said. "My father has seen to every detail of the ceremony. All I have to do is show up, say the words, and everything he's been planning for the last century will fall into place."

"That sounds—"

"Like a prison," she finished flatly.

I swallowed hard. It might have sounded horrible to her. But to me, it sounded like heaven. To have everything done for me, not to have to worry about my next meal, or what my mother had planned, or if Lady Hargate would try to beat me for mopping the hardwood floors with the wrong soap—any kind of life that didn't involve anything close to what I experienced now—

That would be bliss.

All at once, I heard a shout from the other end of the market and a scream of surprise.

A runaway horse, its rider nowhere in sight, thundered towards us, its hooves slammed against the cobblestones. Panic surged through the crowd, but Kristabella seemed frozen in place, her face a mask of terror as it careened through the market.

"Kristabella! Move!" I shouted. My chest was tight, and my heart pounded against my ribs. But she didn't react, her body paralyzed with fear.

With a burst of adrenaline-fueled strength, I launched myself at Kristabella and pushed her out of the way. We tumbled into the flower stall and fell to the cobblestones. The fragrant blooms rained down around us as the horse raced past, its wild eyes filled with panic.

"Are you all right?" I gasped as we lay sprawled on the dirty cobblestones, my body trembling from the exertion.

"Y-yes," Kristabella stammered, her breath coming in ragged gasps. "You saved my life, Lyra. I don't know how to thank you."

"It's... it's nothing," I said, helping her to her feet, my heart swelling with satisfaction. I had risked my life for her, and in doing so had gained her trust—or so I hoped.

"From this day forward, you are more than a friend to me," Kristabella declared as we brushed the dirt from our clothes. She plucked one of the dark flowers from the street and tucked it into my hair before she leaned forward and pressed a kiss to my cold cheek. "I will never forget what you've done for me," she whispered.

"Nor will I," I murmured, my thoughts already racing ahead to the next phase of my plan.

With Kristabella seeing me as a loyal and devoted friend, I was one step closer to achieving my ultimate goal: the love and attention of General Thorne.

But for now, I concealed my true intentions beneath a mask of warmth and gratitude. The game was far from over.

Three

"**M**other!"

My shout filled the house as I rushed through the front door. Dawn was approaching with quick fingers, and my heart pounded with victory.

I had done it. I had found a way to get closer to the General... almost by accident. I couldn't have planned it better myself.

"Mother?"

"In the garden—"

Her voice was faint, but I straightened my shoulders and smoothed down my hair as though she could see me already. She expected me to be neat at all times, there was no telling who would be watching, or who might be visiting even at this late hour.

My cheeks were hot and I pressed the back of my hands against them in an attempt to cool the flush I felt.

The doors that led out to the garden were open and I took a deep breath to steady myself before I stepped out into the morning air.

"Mother? It's late—"

She stood with her back to me, staring up at the dark stones of the fortress as the first light of the rising sun crept up the high wall.

"And you're just coming home," she replied.

"You'll never believe what happened," I said in a rush. "Kristabella—"

"Lady Palimenteri," my mother snapped.

"Yes," I said. "Lady Palimenteri— She asked me to—"

"*Why* would you speak to Lady Palimenteri?"

I paused, taken aback by the sharpness of her tone. "I—"

"You should be speaking to the General," she said as she turned to me. My mother's expression was unreadable, her gaze icy and penetrating as she stared at me.

"But— If I am close to her, then I will be in the General's path," I choked out.

"Your understanding of strategy seems to be lacking, Lyra," my mother said with a hint of disdain in her voice. "You want to approach the General indirectly when you should be seeking him out directly. He is not a man who can be won over through intermediaries. He must see you, hear you, and become interested in you on his own."

"I understand that, Mother," I said, my voice shaking with frustration. "But it's not that simple."

My mother's eyes narrowed. "Nothing worth accomplishing is ever *simple*, Lyra. If you want to win the heart of the General and secure your place in society, you must be willing to do whatever it takes."

"I am," I said resolutely, my anger starting to simmer beneath the surface.

My mother's expression softened slightly as she regarded me with something akin to pity. "Lyra... You know I love you, don't you?"

"Yes," I replied warily.

"And because I love you, I must be honest with you," she said gently. "The General is a powerful man, but he is also a dangerous one. You must tread carefully."

"I— I will," I said. "You have to trust me, mother. I *will* find a way to win the General's affections."

"Affection," my mother scoffed. "You must awaken his *lust*, girl. A warrior needs something to conquer. Lady Palimenteri is an ornament. Nothing more."

I straightened my shoulders as she stepped closer. "Then I shouldn't have any trouble putting my plans into motion," I said firmly.

"No," my mother said softly. "You shouldn't." She walked past me and stepped into the house. "Come inside, the sun is rising quickly. You should be in bed."

My hands tightened into fists at my side. "Yes, Mother," I whispered through gritted teeth.

$\sim$

As much as my mother's ire stung, she wasn't wrong. I knew she thought I was wasting my time, but my role as Kristabella's companion would elevate my own status in the fortress, and lifted our family just a little higher. I knew my mother wouldn't see the merit in it—not at first—but things would change. She was desperate for prestige and power, and I was the key to achieving it.

The General wouldn't look twice at a servant girl with a mop, but as his betrothed's constant companion, he would have no choice but to see me.

The first change was the biggest—Kristabella had demanded that I move into her chambers.

"Thank you for accepting my invitation, Lyra," Kristabella said softly as I brought my meager possessions to her luxurious apartments. Her gray eyes were filled with warmth as she opened the door for me. "It means more to me than you could ever know."

"Of course, my Lady," I replied, trying to mask my growing unease. "I am honored by your trust in me."

"You must only call me Kristabella, now," she said with a firm smile.

"Of course my—"

She frowned briefly and I laughed to see it. "Kristabella," I finished.

"There, that was not so hard," she said.

"No."

"We will spend some time with the seamstress," she said briskly as I set my possessions down upon the narrow bed that had been brought into her chambers for me. "You will require some new gowns. You won't be sweeping stone floors any longer."

"I—"

I hadn't given any thought to my wardrobe, but my cheeks burned with embarrassment as I realized how great the distance between us really was.

"Don't waste a thought on it," Kristabella said quickly. "I have already planned everything. You cannot refuse." She took my hands in hers and squeezed my fingers. "Please."

"You are too kind to me," I said. "I have not been here five minutes and I am already overwhelmed."

"Good," she said with a smile. "Then we must not keep her waiting."

Kristabella and I spent hours with the seamstress and I could only stare in awe at the beautiful silks and fabrics that were laid out for us to choose from, but I let Kristabella do everything. I let her select the colors that would look best, the shape of the neckline that would be most flattering... She knew better than I did what would make me beautiful. All I could think about, with every fluttering length of silk that was fitted to my curves, was how the General would feel when he looked at me. How my beauty would stir him. How he would think of me when I had left his presence...

In the hours before dawn, Kristabella took me to her private library and we spent our time exploring her vast collection of books, discussing art and music, and sharing our most intimate secrets. I couldn't help but notice how her heart-shaped face seemed to carry a shadow of sadness beneath its poised exterior.

Finally, as the rising sun painted the sky with a pale glow of warning, she finally revealed the true reason for her melancholy.

"Lyra, I must confide in you something that weighs heavily on my heart," she began, her voice trembling with emotion. "My wedding is approaching at a faster pace than I could have anticipated... and I find that I cannot bear the thought of it."

"But why? Do you not wish to marry him?"

"I do not wish it," she whispered. Tears glistened in her pale eyes as she shook her head. "And I will not be forced into a marriage that will only serve to strengthen my family's political ties."

I was shocked by her defiance and her willingness to throw off her duty... While I— My duty weighed heavily upon my mind. My own ambition writhed in my chest, but I could not help the sting of pity I felt for my new friend. Even though I was bound to betray her, I could not deny that I was fond of her.

"Tell me that you understand," she begged. Her gray eyes met mine, searching for reassurance. I didn't know what to say, but I took hold of her hand and held it gently.

"Kristabella, I—"

But before I could say anything, she pressed her lips to mine. The kiss was tender, and at first, I hesitated, unsure of my motives, but I didn't pull away. Kristabella's eyes drifted closed and my mouth opened under hers as she teased my lips with her tongue.

As our mouths explored each other, I began to see this encounter as an opportunity to manipulate her, to bend her will to ensure her marriage to General Thorne.

Encouraged by my submission, Kristabella ran her hands through my hair, pulling me closer as the heat of our kisses mounted. It was easy to give in to her, easy to let her believe that she was seducing me.

Our passion ignited like wildfire, our hands roaming over each other's bodies in a desperate dance of desire. Kristabella's breath hitched in her throat as I trailed kisses down her neck and allowed her to guide my hands to her breasts.

"Touch me, Lyra," she moaned, her voice strained with lust. I obliged eagerly and tugged at the laces that held her bodice closed until it loosened enough to allow me to suckle at her hard pink nipples.

She moaned and pressed closer to me as I teased and tormented her with my tongue and the sharpness of my teeth against her tender flesh.

Her breathing grew fast and labored as I pushed one hand up under her embroidered velvet skirts and brushed my fingers against the slick heat between her legs.

"Yes," she hissed as she rocked her hips forward, urging me to slide my fingers into her silken depths. Kristabella gripped my shoulder as she rode my hand, begging me without words to bring her to climax. My thumb pressed against her clit to make her gasp as I pumped my fingers deep inside her.

Kristabella's nails dug into my flesh as she gasped and her body trembled with pleasure. Every touch, every sound only fueled my own desire, and I found myself lost in a sea of lust and manipulation as Kristabella's climax crashed over her. Her cries echoed in the stone chamber as she clung to me, shaking, as the sensations swept her away.

I kissed her breasts, licking and sucking gently at her aching nipples as she leaned against me, breathing hard as the tide of pleasure ebbed away.

"It's almost dawn," I murmured as I drew my fingers gently from her soaking haven. She moaned as I pushed my fingers into her mouth, forcing her to suck her own sweet juices from my digits. When she had licked them clean I took hold of her chin and kissed her hard, tasting her sweetness on her lips and tongue and leaving her breathless before I tied the laces of her bodice once more.

She moaned again as I set my hands on her hips.

"We should go," I said softly. "The morning—"

Kristabella nodded and pushed herself to her feet before she reached down to help me stand. Her fingers twined with mine as she smiled and pulled me out of the library and down the corridor toward the chambers we now shared.

As soon as the door closed behind us, Kristabella's lips were on mine once more.

This time I didn't hold back and returned her passion with my own.

She pulled back just enough to smile at me as she tugged at the hastily tied laces at the front of her gown. "Come to bed," she whispered.

I didn't have to be asked twice and fumbled with the laces of my own bodice until the fabric fell away from my body and I could peel away the layers of fabric between us until we stood naked before each other.

Kristabella took me in her arms and held me tightly as she kissed my neck. "Do you want this as much as I do?"

I answered her by pressing my lips to hers in a heated kiss that left her breathless. I had to make her think that I wanted her as much as she wanted me. I did, of course, I couldn't deny the lust that coursed through my veins like fire... but I would do anything to make her believe that I wanted more.

This was how I would undo her hold on the General. This was how I could manipulate her to achieve my heart's desire.

A shiver ran through me as Kristabella grabbed hold of my hands and pulled me toward the enormous bed. The thick velvet curtains had been closed by a maid earlier in the evening in anticipation of the rising sun, and I could see the steady glow of our ancient enemy behind the thick brocade as it burned its way through the sky.

On any other day I would have been at home with my mother,

huddled in my bedchamber while I hoped that my curtains were enough to keep the sun's harmful rays at bay.

But here in the fortress I was safe.

Kristabella pushed me back onto the bed and she smiled as I bounced on the soft mattress. I bit back a moan as my body sank into the unfamiliar decadence of the feather coverlet.

Without hesitation, Kristabella climbed up onto the bed and pinned me down as she straddled my hips and then brushed her fingertips over my breasts.

"You're so beautiful," she whispered as she rolled one nipple between her thumb and forefinger and drew it to a hard peak.

I rewarded her ministrations with a low hiss of pleasure as I bent over and flicked her tongue across my erect nipple before she took it into her mouth and suckled it gently.

Her hands moved leisurely over the planes of my body, teasing every inch of skin until gooseflesh rose in a wave of heat between my thighs. My face burned under her heated gaze as I tangled my hands in her hair and held her close as she licked and nipped at my breasts until I was gasping with lust.

My entire body ached with need for her touch when she pulled away from my breasts and slid lower until I moaned in desperate desire. Her lips parted just long enough to brush against the curve of my hip before she settled between my thighs, teasing the tender flesh of my inner thighs with flicks of her tongue but never committing to tasting the honey of my pussy. Frustrated by her teasing, I buried my hands in her hair again and tugged just hard enough to draw a moan from her lips that sent a jolt of pleasure straight to the center of my core as I pulled her mouth against my aching pussy.

Kristabella's hands gripped my thighs as she spread my legs further apart and parted my slick pink folds with one finger. I bit down hard on my lip and tasted blood as I moaned.

"Please—"

Her soft chuckle fluttered over my heated skin and I lifted my hips to force her mouth onto my slick cleft.

"Greedy girl," she murmured, but then her mouth was sealed upon me and her tongue stroked between my folds like an inferno that threatened to engulf me whole.

Every searing swipe of her tongue was consuming, melting all thoughts of duty or revenge or shame away until there was only her and the warm fingers of fire building inside me.

"Kristabella..." My voice was barely more than a whisper, a gasp, but she seemed to understand because she moaned around my flesh in response. Slowly, patiently, she teased me higher and higher until there was no retreat from the inferno. By the time she slid her fingers inside me, there was no thought of anything but the rolling tide of pleasure that crested inside me, and then overflowed and crashed out of control.

I cried her name again as I rode the wave, clutching at the sheets as if to claw my way back from the abyss. She lapped and suckled at my clit as I shattered, my hips bucked as the movement of her fingers drove me even higher with every touch of her mouth against the throbbing center of my bliss before she finally pulled away and sat up with a smile on her lips.

"Come here," I groaned as I released my grip on her hair and pulled her toward me.

She chuckled and crawled up beside me to lie against my shoulder. "I'm not finished yet," she murmured as she trailed a hand down my body.

I groaned against her mouth when her fingers dipped lower still to brush against the tender flesh between my legs. Her breath caught in her throat as she felt how hot and wet I was, and how ready I was to have her again.

Kristabella's mouth claimed mine as her fingers rubbed against my swollen clit and worked it until I was gasping for breath and writhing against her, desperate for release.

With a groan I laid my hands on Kristabella's hips and pulled her over me. I held onto her ass hard and urged her into the cradle formed by my thighs until I felt her hot cleft press eagerly against mine.

With a moan that echoed from both of our lips, we joined together. Slowly at first, testing each other, we began to move. A gentle rocking of our hips, intensified by the slickness of our arousal, created a delicious friction that made us both gasp. I rocked my hips harder and harder as Kristabella moaned, setting a rhythm that left us both breathless as we drove each other toward the pinnacle of pleasure.

Kristabella cried out as she came, and I pulled her down to kiss me as her wetness flooded over me and as I claimed her mouth my own climax rushed forward and I shuddered against her, gasping with the intensity of it.

She collapsed against me, her body trembling as she laughed softly.

"That was—"

"Hush," I murmured as I stroked my hand over her tangled hair.

We lay together on her bed, hearts racing, breath ragged, our skin hot and tingling while my mind raced with the possibilities this new closeness could unlock.

"Would you be jealous if I married him?" she asked suddenly, her gray eyes studying my face intently.

My thoughts were frantic.

What would she want to hear?

What would I want to hear?

"Yes," I confessed, feeling a thrill of power knowing that my admission fueled her desire for me. "But I... I care for you too deeply to let my selfishness stand in the way of your marriage."

"Prove it," she whispered, her lips brushing against mine as she pressed her body closer.

Our mouths met in a searing kiss, her tongue slipping past my lips as her hands roamed over my naked flesh, reigniting the fire within me. I surrendered myself to her touch, allowing myself to be consumed by our passionate dance once more.

Our bodies moved together in perfect harmony, the sound of our moans and sighs echoing through the luxurious chamber. Kristabella's fingers trailed down my spine and sent shivers of pleasure coursing through me as I reveled in the sensation of control that coursed through my veins.

"Tell me you want me," she whispered into my ear, her breath hot and desperate as I slid my fingers inside her.

"Always," I growled, my desire for her an undeniable force that threatened to consume us both.

As her climax claimed her, I knew that I had taken the first step toward gaining Kristabella's trust.

As Kristabella's breathing steadied and her body relaxed, I knew she had succumbed to the embrace of sleep. The warmth of her naked form pressed against mine was intoxicating, but my mind raced with thoughts that refused to be silenced.

My heart fluttered at the memory of our passionate exchange, the raw intensity of our lustful exploration sent shivers down my spine and I replayed the desperate hunger in her eyes as she asked if I would be jealous of her marrying the General. My admission had only served to fuel her desire, but my only jealousy was imagining her in the General's bed instead of me.

"Would you really be jealous?" Kristabella murmured in her sleep, a soft smile gracing her lips.

"Of course," I whispered into her ear, wondering if she could hear me within the depths of her dreams.

In the quiet darkness, I contemplated how best to manipulate Kristabella into proceeding with her marriage to General Thorne. Although it pained me to think of their bond being sealed, I knew that it was the only way I could get close to the General.

Four

Being Kistabella's companion meant that we spent almost every moment of every day together, but it was the moments that we were truly alone that, against my own judgment, I had come to crave.

In the garden one night, under the light of a moon that was bold enough to glow through the clouds that rolled overhead.

"Tell me, Lyra," she whispered as her fingers traced the delicate petals of a rose, "what is the most *wicked* thing you've ever done?"

I hesitated, feeling my heart race at the memory of my darkest secret, but the intensity of her gaze drew me in like a moth to a flame. "Once, when I was younger, I seduced a man twice my age, just to see the look of shame in his eyes afterwards."

It was a lie, of course, but Kristabella didn't need to know that.

A wicked grin spread across her lips, and she stepped closer, her breath hot against my ear. "You really are a naughty girl."

My body trembled as her words sent a shiver down my spine. It was in these intimate moments that I found myself becoming increasingly enraptured by Kristabella. The way her pale eyes glinted with mischief, her laughter like music in the air, made my desire for her burn hotter than any fire. Though my mind screamed at me for forsaking the promises I had made to my mother, my heart couldn't help but ache for her touch.

She pushed me back into the shadows of the rose bushes and kissed me hard as her hands roamed over my breasts.

"Will you let me taste you," she murmured against my lips.

"Yes," I whispered.

Without hesitation she sank down to her knees in the grass and ducked beneath my skirts.

I gasped as her fingers dug into the yielding flesh of my thighs, forcing them apart. "You smell delicious," she said, her voice muffled by the fabric of my gown.

One of her long fingers slid between my folds, teasing against my clit before she teased it against my entrance.

My breaths came in short gasps as her tongue followed the path of her fingers as she brought me closer and closer to release.

It wasn't fair, I thought to myself frantically, wishing that I could look into her eyes as she took me apart.

No breeze teased my heated skin, only Kristabella's breath on my body as her lips possessed me. Her tongue circled around my clit as her fingers stroked deep inside of me, first one and then two and three as she tormented me and dared me to cry out loud.

But I couldn't. I couldn't alert the guards that waited nearby even though I was certain that they turned a blind eye to our stolen kisses and caresses.

Kristabella's tongue worked my clit with expert strokes and my back arched against the stone wall with the intensity of the pleasure that tore through me as she brought me closer and closer to orgasm.

I bit down hard on my lip to keep from crying out. The last thing I wanted was for us to be discovered in the moonlit garden, but Kristabella seemed more than eager to test my resolve. Her fingers were tight on my thighs and I knew that her grip would leave bruises. My hips bucked forward as I rode her tongue and finally let myself go as the sharpness of my climax cut through my senses.

My fingertips scraped against the stones as my body arched and Kristabella's moan of triumph vibrated against my throbbing pussy as she lapped up the flood of wetness that she had caused.

I moaned softly as she pulled her mouth away from my soaking cleft and emerged from beneath my skirts. Her full lips were painted with my juices and I grabbed her shoulders and pulled her close to kiss her and tasted myself on her mouth and tongue.

"You're too delicious for words," she murmured with a small smile when I finally released her.

"we have to be careful," I whispered back. "What if someone saw us?"

"What about it?"

"You are betrothed to General Valerius," I hissed back.

"And?"

I didn't know how to respond to that but Kristabella grabbed hold of my hand and didn't give me a chance to reply. "Come," she said. "I have some new books to show you. My father just had them delivered to the library..."

I followed her obediently, but my mind was whirling with possibilities—what would the General think if he knew about our clandestine affair? Would it make him think twice about their approaching marriage?

I had hoped that by spending more time with Kristabella that I would see the General more often—but he was often away from the fortress and I had only caught a few glimpses of him since I had moved into Kristabella's chambers.

If I wanted to keep my promise to my mother, and to myself, I would have to change that... sooner than later.

～

One evening as I walked to Kristabella's chambers, I was determined to find a way to speak to the General. With every step I took, I grew more determined. My position as Kristabella's companion had changed many things for me—he would grant me an audience if I requested it. I was sure of that.

The door to Kristabella's chamber was open, and I paused in the corridor as I heard voices.

A shiver rippled up my spine as I recognized the sensual rumble of the General's voice.

I couldn't hear what they were talking about, but Kristabella's tone sounded sharp. As I moved closer I tried to keep my footsteps as silent as possible on the stone floor.

"You can't expect that," Kristabella said coldly.

"It is not a matter of expectation, my Lady," the General replied. "It is duty."

"Get out," Kristabella said. "I shall tell my father that you have come here—"

"Tell him whatever you like," the General said, and I could hear the smile in his dark voice. My stomach tightened at the sound of it.

"What—"

"Your father has already given his permission," he said. There was a stunned silence that followed these words and I pressed myself against the wall as the echo of the General's boots filled the air as he strode toward the open door.

He stepped into the corridor and my breath caught in my throat as his dark eyes swept over me.

"Lyra," he said.

"General," I murmured as I inclined my head.

He stepped close to me and placed his fingers beneath my chin and forced me to look at him.

"She's upset," he said softly. "Comfort her."

"Of course," I choked out.

"You know what duty is, do you not?"

I swallowed hard. "I do."

His smile showed a flash of sharp teeth. "Good. Perhaps you can talk some sense into her."

He released his gentle grip on my chin and stepped away. He walked down the corridor without a backward glance and I fought to take a steady breath to calm my pounding heart.

What could they have been speaking about that would upset her so much? Had she told him that she did not wish to be married to him? The mention of duty—

I rubbed my hands over my face and then pushed my hands through my hair. I straightened my shoulders and walked toward the open door of Kristabella's bedchamber.

She stood by the window, the last rays of the setting sun cast an ethereal glow on her heart-shaped face and curling black hair. Her gray eyes met mine as she turned to me, and a strange heat rose within my chest.

"Kristabella," I began, my voice wavering. "Is everything alright?"

"It isn't," she said tersely. "But now that you're here—"

"What happened?"

"It— The General— What did you hear?"

"Nothing," I said quickly. "Only raised voices—"

Kristabella made a face. "The General was here to... assert himself."

I didn't know what that meant, but Kristabella seemed more angry than upset.

"Is there anything I can do?" I asked as she walked toward me.

As she reached out to touch my hand, I faltered and my words caught in my throat. Kristabella's expression shifted, her eyes narrowing ever so slightly.

"Perhaps there is something you can do," she said.

"Really?" My mind raced with what she could possibly have in mind.

"An arrangement," she clarified, her pale gaze never leaving mine. "One that would secure your family's future while allowing us to remain close."

"I— I don't understand." My heartbeat quickened with a mixture of apprehension and hope.

"The General has made it clear to me that he intends to consummate our union before the wedding night."

"But—"

"He has already spoken to my father," Kristabella said briskly. "It is... frowned upon, but not unusual, especially for someone of the General's status."

"I— I don't understand—"

Kristabella's smile was soft as she stroked a finger down my cheek. "I don't think I have to ask if you find the General attractive... Do I?"

I swallowed hard. "Kristabella—"

"I want you to join General Valerius and I in our... intimate affairs," she said, her voice low and seductive. "He has made it clear to me that he desires more than I am willing to give... But I cannot bear to part with you. This way, we all get what we desire."

My heart pounded wildly in my chest, both shocked and intrigued by her proposition. Kristabella's gray eyes were filled with dominance and determination, and I knew she would not take no for an answer lightly.

"Kristabella, I..." I stammered, my conflicting emotions threatening to overwhelm me.

This was what I wanted—deep down.

But I couldn't help the fear that crept into my mind.

Did she suspect my true motives?

Was this a trap?

"Just promise me that you'll think about it, Lyra," she urged. Her fingers traced a delicate pattern on the back of my hand that sent shivers up my spine. "We could have everything. Security, power... All you need to do is accept."

As I stared into her eyes, I felt torn between desire and duty, passion and principle. This was not what I had envisioned for our relationship, nor was it something I had ever considered before. And yet, a part of me longed for the freedom, and the pleasure that Kristabella's proposal promised.

If I could manipulate both her and the General at the same time—

I nodded. "I will think about it," I whispered.

"Good," she replied, her gaze softening slightly. "But remember, Lyra, time is a luxury we may not always have."

I gave myself three days to pretend to consider Kristabella's request.

I ached to tell my mother about it—but I did not know if I could bear her judgments. Or her machinations, which would surely follow. I wanted to prove to her that I could manage my own future—our future—without her interference.

It was easier to allow her to believe that I was failing, or wasting time rather than giving her the satisfaction of knowing that I needed her help.

I didn't need her help.

I wanted this.

As soon as the words had left her lips, it had taken all of my will not to shout my response.

Yes.

A thousand times, yes.

It was everything I had ever wanted. Kristabella's proposal would set me not just in the General's eye... but in his bed. Where I belonged.

Kristabella respected my request for time to think about her offer and over the three days she didn't mention the General, or his demands, at all.

With each night that passed, I wanted to tell her.

So many moments.

Finally, I decided that I had pretended long enough.

We were seated in the fortress library, leaning against each other as we read. but I had read the same paragraph more than seven times by the time I found enough courage to speak.

"Kristabella," I said, my voice steadier than I thought possible. "I've made my decision."

She closed her book and set it aside. Her gray eyes were serious as they met mine.

"I— I accept your invitation."

"Ah, Lyra," she purred as she leaned toward me. "I'm so pleased to hear it."

Kristabella's fingers brushed against my cheek before trailing down my throat. Her touch sent shivers of anticipation coursing through my veins. She pressed her lips against mine, and I surrendered to the passion that flared between us. The taste of her was intoxicating and irresistible.

She pulled away and took hold of my hands. She squeezed my fingers gently before she drew them to her lips and kissed my knuckles gently.

"You have made me very happy," she whispered. "I promise you, Lyra—this will change nothing between us."

"You won't— you won't be jealous?"

She smiled, but it was brief. "I asked you if you would be jealous when I married the General..."

"But won't you be jealous?" I asked.

Her smile was smooth and seductive. "I will enjoy every moment of watching your pleasure—but you have to promise me something."

"Anything," I said before I could stop myself.

Too eager.

But her eyes brightened and I knew I had said what she wanted to hear.

"Your climax—your ecstasy... *That belongs to me.*"

Her gray eyes held mine.

Unwavering.

"Promise me," she hissed as she squeezed my fingers.

Tight enough to make my breath catch with the flash of pain that accompanied the pressure of her grip.

"I— I promise," I choked out.

She kissed me again.

Hard.

I froze in place, eyes squeezed shut tight as she claimed my mouth and thrust her tongue between my lips, forcing me to open my mouth.

Her kiss was hungry and possessive and I couldn't help the way that my body responded to her.

Kristabella dragged her mouth down my jaw and nipped at the side of my neck, grazing my flesh with the sharpness of her teeth. She had never drunk from me—never claimed me in that way.

"This is the only way we can be together," she murmured against my throat.

"I know," I whispered as I pulled her into my arms.

I was on the precipice of everything I wanted—everything I had ever hoped for. Everything I had hungered for... and for some reason, I was reluctant to take it.

Five

I didn't know when Kristabella's proposal would take effect, or what I could expect from such an arrangement. Had the General been informed of his arrangement? Or would it be a surprise to him?

But more importantly—would it be a surprise that he would welcome?

For weeks it felt as though I was walking on broken glass.

Every side-eyed glance. Every whisper in the corridor.

Each time Kristabella and I shared her bed I worried that something would happen—that we would be discovered, or, that I would be dragged away and shamed for my brazen attempt at what could only be labeled as treason.

Was it treason?

I wanted the General for my own, and I didn't care how that would be achieved—only that I would achieve it.

But my affection and my desire for Kristabella was impossible to ignore.

My lust for the General would bring me power and prestige... but what I felt for her—

No.

I had a duty to fulfill.

A promise I had made.

Duty and desire were not the same.

But what if they could be?

My mother would not need to know—she would only know when I had completed my task and Kristabella had been set aside.

As the moon rose and spilled its silver light over the bed I dragged my fingers over Kristabella's smooth skin. A washtub filled with steaming water had been brought into the room by servants who wouldn't look at us—so much the better.

I still wasn't comfortable enough to feel untouchable in my new position. It would take nothing at all for me to be cast back into the ranks of servants who worked in the fortress—or worse, cast out into the streets.

Kristabella moved against me, her smile was sensual and slow as she cuddled against my breasts. "Did they bring washing water?"

"Mmm," I hummed as she lifted her chin to kiss me.

"Come, then, let us prepare for our evening," she murmured as she slid out of the warmth of the bed and walked over to the washtub.

I rolled over onto my stomach to watch her as she stepped into the hot water and smiled as she dipped a piece of clean linen into the water and drew it over her naked body. Droplets of scented water rolled down over the tawny perfection of her skin and left tantalizing trails down her full breasts and the planes of her hips.

"Come," she urged. Her quick smile flashed sharp teeth at me, the gray eyes bright with mirth.

"Don't keep me waiting, Lyra."

I slid off the bed and walked toward her with languid steps. Kristabella's hands slid over her nakedness and one dipped between her legs, purposefully teasing her clit so that I could watch her.

"Shall I help you wash, my Lady?" I murmured as I stepped into the washtub with her. Kristabella's breath caught as I pressed my lips against the side of her neck and allowed my teeth to graze against her damp skin.

The delicate scent of the water mixed with the tang of our pleasure-tinged sweat and the heady perfume of it made my pussy clench.

My hands trailed over Kristabella's body, purposefully allowing my fingers to slide down between her legs, even as my heart fluttered nervously against my ribs.

Dozens of Union Regents had committed crimes against our race—and many more had performed acts far more perverted than what we were doing in the privacy of Kristabella's bedchamber, but that didn't stop me from worrying—

If we were caught—could I somehow turn it to my advantage? Could I convince whoever discovers us that I had been coerced into these acts?

But, in truth, there was no coercion... I wanted this as much as she did. Our relationship had begun as a lie, as a manipulation, but I couldn't deny how much I craved Kristabella's touch and the taste of her...

Our bodies melded together, hands exploring each other's curves and crevices, mouths hungrily devouring one another. The air around us crackled with energy, our moans and gasps a symphony of lust and desire.

As Kristabella's fingers teased my throbbing core, the door to her chamber creaked open.

I gasped in fear and surprise and would have fallen, but Kristabella caught me and held me fast.

Lust pounded in my veins, but it was quickly being replaced by fear. "Kristbella—"

"Hush," she hissed. Her gray eyes narrowed as she stared at the door. "Who goes there," she called out.

"Lady Palimenteri, I hope I haven't caught you at a—"

I choked back a cry as General Thorne Valerius stepped into the chamber. His dark eyes locked onto us and I recognized a predatory hunger lurking within their depths that made my pussy throb.

"Not at all, General," Kristabella said smoothly. "Won't you join us?" Kristabella's voice was heavy with arousal and I swallowed hard as she rubbed her hand over my breast and plucked at my already hard nipple to make me gasp.

"What—"

"Lyra has agreed to be our plaything," she said, interrupting him. "We will share her... Does that please you?"

The General's eyebrow rose slightly. "This is your idea, my Lady?"

"It is," she replied firmly. "This way we can *both* have what we want. If you wish to go through with this marriage, then you will fuck her instead of me..."

I licked my lips and moaned as Kristabella's other hand slid between my thighs and her fingers teased against my swollen clit.

"She's already wet," Kristabella whispered.

The general's dark gaze flickered to me. "And you consent to this?" he asked me.

"I—" A moan choked my words as a shudder of pleasure rippled through my body. "I do," I gasped.

Thorne approached us slowly, and I could see the outline of his cock against his leather breeches. My breath hissed between my teeth as Kristabella pinched my nipple hard enough to make my back arch. Her fingers strummed against my clit, driving powerful sensations through my body—the intensity of the pleasure that coursed through me made me helpless as the General stood in front of us.

The General unpinned his cloak and tossed it aside. "This is your compromise?"

"It is," Kristabella replied. She pressed her lips to the side of my throat and looked into the General's eyes. "Is this arrangement to your liking?"

The General regarded me carefully, watching me shudder with pleasure in Kristabella's grip. Then he nodded. "It is."

"Good girl," Kristabella purred in my ear as I moaned louder.

The General pulled his tunic over his head and threw it onto the floor alongside his cloak.

Bare-chested, he stepped closer and brushed his fingers over my jaw and over my bottom lip.

"Beautiful," he murmured. His hand dragged down my body and his fingers circled my other breast, kneading it gently before he bent his head to suckle the hard peak of my nipple.

I moaned as his teeth scraped against the tender flesh, driving my lust even higher.

Kristabella's fingers teased against my entrance, dipping inside as the General's powerful hands slid over my wet skin and between my thighs. He grunted as his fingers rubbed against my swollen clit and I arched back against Kristabella who held me steady.

"Take her to the bed," he growled.

I choked on my moan of disappointment as the assault on my senses ended abruptly.

Kristabella helped me out of the washtub, and I walked on unsteady legs toward the bed. Kristabella crawled onto the soft mattress and lay back upon the pillows. She spread her legs and beckoned for me to follow her.

I was hungry for her, my mind a whirl of lust and desire and I climbed up onto the bed, held prisoner by her gray eyes and sensual smile.

"Remember what belongs to me," she purred as she ran her hands through my hair and then tightened her grip as she pulled my eager mouth toward her slick pussy.

"Yes," I murmured.

I remembered what she had said, and her words thundered through my mind as my pussy throbbed.

Your pleasure belongs to me.

"Good girl," she murmured as I stroked my hands along Kristabella's soft thighs and pushed her legs further apart, opening her to me.

"So beautiful," I whispered as I pressed light kisses along her tender flesh and inhaled her sweet musk. She was intoxicating, and I wanted to make her moan loud enough to fill the chamber with the sounds of her pleasure.

I tasted her hungrily, my tongue sliding through her folds before I sucked at her clit and made her back arch.

My fingers teased at her entrance and she moaned and tugged on my hair, holding me against her pussy as I lapped at her sweetness.

I had almost forgotten that the General was in the room, but his groan sent a shiver down my spine and I arched my back, pushing my ass higher into the air as I devoured Kristabella's sweet cunt.

She writhed on the bed under me as the General's fingers slid over the curve of my ass and the thick head of his cock pressed against my aching entrance.

"Fuck her, Thorne," Kristabella moaned as I teased her with my tongue and then pushed it inside her.

He didn't need any other encouragement.

Without hesitation, the General's cock thrust deep into my hot flesh, filling me completely as he groaned.

I cried out as his cock slammed into me and the sensations exploded across my nerve endings. I pushed two fingers into Kristabella's velvet softness and mimicked the pace of the General's thrusts with my hand.

She cried out, writhing and shuddering as I fucked her with my fingers even as the General's thick cock pounded into my eager pussy. Kristabella's cunt clenched around my fingers and she cried out as she came, hard and fast, and I moaned as I tasted her climax on my tongue.

A moment later, Kristabella's fingers tightened in my hair as she pulled me away from her soaking haven.

"Remember your purpose," she purred as she pulled me toward her. She released her hold on my hair, and I groaned as the General's cock slid from my pussy. I looked back over my shoulder at him. His smile was languid as he stroked his cock, slick with my wetness.

Kristabella dug her nails into my shoulder.

"Look at me," she hissed.

I did as I was commanded and met her pale gaze as boldly as I could.

"Good girl," she murmured. "You're mine, remember?"

"Yes, my Lady," I whispered. I shuddered under her touch and moaned as she rose up and reached between my thighs to push two fingers inside my dripping pussy. Pain and pleasure mingled in a delectable mix that made me gasp. "He stretched you," she murmured in my ear. "Do you like being used like this?"

"Yes," I moaned.

She pulled me against her and forced my thighs wider apart with her knees as she slid her fingers through the juices that dripped from my aching pussy. I bit down hard on my lip as she spread the slickness of my arousal between my ass cheeks and over the contour of my anus. My muscles clenched in surprise—both in fear and excitement—and then relaxed at her gentle coaxing only to clench again when the General groaned.

"He's going to take you here, too," Kristabella murmured. She kissed me as her fingers rubbed the slick juices against the puckered ring protecting my entrance and teased inside, stretching it—preparing me for the more intense pleasure that was to come.

"Are you ready?" she whispered.

I bit my lip and nodded. "Yes—"

With a grunt, the General pushed his cock between Kristabella's fingers and forced them open so he could fuck me with slow strokes that stretched my flesh slowly around the thick head of his big cock. Kristabella held me tight as I shook.

At first, it was painful, a raw and primal feeling that made me want to pull away, but I couldn't move. Kristabella held me tight, crooning in my ear as she held me steady for the General.

It was like nothing I'd ever experienced before—the sensations of pain and pleasure blended together until they were indistinguishable from each other.

Between the two of them, they had me helpless to their whims —helpless to the pleasure that coursed through me and threatened to rob me of my sanity.

"That's it," Kristabella purred. "Take every inch of him."

The General's strokes were smooth and slow, allowing me to become used to the sensation until I began to crave it.

I moaned and gasped as I clung to Kristabella's shoulder, and she encouraged me with kisses and caresses that drove me even closer to climax. She slid two fingers into my pussy, thrusting deep and slow in time with the General's movements.

It took everything in me not to fall there on top of her and beg for more—to beg for Kristabella's strong hands to grip my hair again or her mouth to clamp down on my clit and her tongue murder me with pleasure...but somehow I managed to hold myself still—to keep from distracting General Thorne as he took full advantage of my submissive body.

"Please," I murmured.

My head rested on Kristabella's shoulder as her fingers slid from my pussy and over the hard nub of my clit. Her other hand still held my ass cheeks apart as the General fucked into me with long, slow strokes, his cock gliding into that forbidden channel at an agonizing pace—slowly pushing me toward the edge of orgasm as Kristabella alternated between rubbing my clit and fucking me with her fingers.

It was too much to bear, and I couldn't hold on any longer.

"Kristabella," I moaned, my voice choked.

"It belongs to me," Kristabella whispered as my body tightened.

She kissed me hard as my orgasm crashed over me, and I

moaned and cried out against her mouth as the General grunted, his steady thrusts losing their rhythm as he came and filled my ass with his hot cum.

"So fucking beautiful," Kristabella growled in my ear as she stroked herself to a shuddering climax beneath us both.

She trailed feathery kisses across the arch of my neck as she held my shuddering body against hers. "You're mine," she whispered in a choked voice.

"Yours," I murmured.

The General withdrew, his hand lingering on my hip for just a moment before he stepped away.

Everything around me blurred and shifted and all I could hear was the soothing murmur of Kristabella's voice in my ear.

I was safe in her arms.

My eyes drifted closed and I relaxed into the delicious throb of my pleasure-filled body.

In the dim light of dawn, I awoke to the sound of the chamber door opening. My eyes fluttered open, and I saw General Thorne's broad back disappear through the doorway.

My body still hummed from the previous night's events and every inch of my skin tingled with the residual pleasure that coursed through my veins like wildfire.

"Did you sleep well?" Kristabella's sultry voice pulled me back into the present as she shifted her naked form beside me. Her gray eyes held mine, a mixture of satisfaction and vulnerability reflected in them.

"Last night... it was..." I struggled to find the words, my mind still foggy with desire and confusion.

"Intense," she finished for me, her fingers tracing delicate patterns on my bare skin. "Yes, it was. But now, we need to talk."

"About what?" I asked, propping myself up on one elbow, my other hand absently stroked along her side.

"About *our* future," Kristabella began, her gaze locked onto mine. "Did you enjoy our little—interlude?"

Her thumb traced over my bottom lip.

"I did," I whispered.

"Do you want more?"

"I want whatever you want," I said. I didn't know what she wanted to hear, but the look in her eyes told me that it was enough.

"Good," she said. "The General enjoyed you... and I know he'll want you again."

Kristabella pushed her thumb into my mouth and I sucked it greedily and she smiled as she pressed the pad of it against my fang. I moaned as the heady sweetness of her blood touched my tongue.

"You will remain close to me, as my lover, and you will also serve as the General's sexual partner. In return, I will give you everything you've ever desired."

Not everything...

The thought streaked through my mind like a fiery comet and I could not ignore the echo of it in my mind.

But this time? This time my ambitious thought was accompanied by a stab of guilt.

Kristabella pulled her thumb from my mouth and kissed me gently. My lips opened under hers and I moaned as she pulled me close.

"Are you certain that you're comfortable with this?" I couldn't help but ask, my thoughts racing as the reality of her proposition sank in.

"Nothing would please me more than to share you with him," Kristabella replied, her eyes darkening with desire. "I want to watch you submit to his power, to see the ecstasy on your face as he takes you. And then, when he's done, I want to claim you as my own once more."

The raw carnality of her words sent shivers down my spine and ignited a lustful fire within me. My mind reeled, struggling to reconcile the passion and excitement that gripped me with the uncertainty and fear that also took root.

"But you must promise me something," she said, gripping my chin tight.

"Anything," I gasped.

"You will never be alone with him," she said. "You will never fuck him without me. Do you understand?" Kristabella asked, her voice laced with anticipation.

I hesitated for a moment, weighing the consequences of my decision.

What about my plan—

"I understand," I murmured.

My mind reeled as Kristabella kissed me hard enough to leave me breathless.

I needed time to think... time to figure out how I could turn this to my advantage.

Six

The moonlight cast a silvery glow on our entwined bodies as Kristabella and I lost ourselves in each other's touch. Our moans filled the air as she explored my body with her mouth and tongue, expertly coaxing my climax to higher and higher peaks.

"Kristabella."

I breathed her name like a prayer, clutching at the soft sheets beneath us. It had been two weeks since our night with the General, and she had said nothing more about it—as though it hadn't happened at all.

But I couldn't forget it, nor could I deny that I wanted more.

Right now, however, Kristabella was the only thing on my mind as my climax crested and rushed through me. Kristabella moaned as I came hard on her tongue.

As my cries echoed off the chamber walls, the wooden door slammed open. The sudden sound jarred me from the world of ecstasy we had created.

My mother, Helena Batherst, stood in the doorway, her face a mask of shock and rage. The heat that had moments ago coursed through my veins was replaced by a cold dread.

"Explain yourself, Lyra!" she demanded, her sharp eyes boring into me with a cold intensity that could rival the northern ice fields.

Kristabella quickly untangled herself from me and grabbed her robe, wrapping it around her lithe form.

"What is the meaning of this?" she demanded.

"My Lady Palimenteri," my mother said with a smooth smile. "I must speak with my daughter, most urgently." Kristabella didn't move, any mother's expression hardened. "It is a... private matter. I'm sure you understand."

Kristabella shot me a pained look before she nodded and slipped out of the room without uttering another word.

I felt a sudden pang that she didn't stay—she had promised to protect me...

Once Kristabella had gone, my mother closed the door behind her and fixed me with a stern glare. "What were you thinking?" my mother hissed as she spun around to face me. "You know your duty to this family, and here I find you, playing the whore to the very woman you're supposed to replace."

Her words cut through me like a knife, reminding me of the precarious position our low-status family held in the court.

"Can you not see the consequences of your actions?" she continued, her voice laced with frustration. "You have jeopardized everything we've worked for, everything I have done for you—and for what? You shame yourself and this family."

I wrapped the sheet around my body, feeling more exposed and vulnerable than ever. I knew she was right—I had been reckless.

"Mother, it's not just—" I whispered, desperately trying to make her understand, even as I knew her disapproval would only deepen. "You have to trust me—I am getting closer to the General—"

"Enough!" she snapped, her voice cold and unyielding. "I have had enough of your lies and delays. You must make a choice, Lyra. Duty to *me*, or to the woman who just abandoned you?"

Her words hung heavily in the air between us and the weight of the decision before me pressed down on my chest until it was hard to breathe.

"Mother, you know I'm loyal to you— You just have to be patient. My plan is working."

My mothers' eyes narrowed, as if she were trying to discern whether I was lying to her or not. "Your thoughts should be set upon capturing the heart of General Thorne Valerius, not between the thighs of that Palimenteri girl."

I swallowed hard and pulled the blanket tighter around my nakedness. "My relationship with Kristabella is all part of the plan," I continued, fighting to keep my voice steady. "I'm using our connection to get close to the General—you have to trust me. Please. I'm so close. I just need more time."

"I do not like delays," she said sternly, but I could see something different in her eyes. "Your duty to your family must come first. You know that as well as I do."

"Of course," I replied through gritted teeth, turning away from her piercing gaze. "I understand."

"Good," she said curtly, her tone softened just slightly. "We cannot afford any mistakes. *You* can't afford any mistakes. You are in a perilous position, but your carnal proclivities might prove advantageous. Use them as they are using you."

Her eyes raked over me and my cheeks burned with shame as I thought of how she had discovered me—in the throes of passion with Kristabella between my thighs.

Without another word, my mother swept out of the room, leaving me alone with my thoughts.

As the door clicked shut behind her, the tears I had been holding back finally spilled over and streamed down my cheeks in a hot, uncontrollable torrent.

My plans seemed so cruel now—could I really do this to Kristabella?

Could I really usurp her position in the General's bed and cast her aside?

I pressed my cold hands to my cheeks and tried to take a steady breath.

My mother was right. I had to focus on what I wanted—but what did I want? What did I *really* want?

I stood outside Kristabella's chamber, my heart pounding and hands shaking as I replayed my mother's words in my mind. I took a deep breath and hoped that my plans hadn't been derailed by my mother's angry discovery... With a hesitant hand, I knocked softly on her door.

"Kristabella, it's Lyra," I whispered, my voice hoarse from the turmoil of emotions swirling within me. "May I come in? I want to talk."

The door swung open with such force that it nearly knocked me over. Kristabella's gray eyes bored into mine, cold and accusatory. "How dare you?" she spat, her voice laced with venom.

"Please, let me explain," I begged, stepping inside her room and closing the door behind me. "My mother— She doesn't under-stand— She's worried about our reputation—"

"Save your worthless lies." Kristabella's face was a mask of fury, her cheeks flushed red. "*I heard everything*–I was listening outside the door while you spoke with your mother."

My heart sank like a stone in water, and I struggled to find words. "Kristabella, I—"

"Did you *really* think you could win General Thorne's favor?" she interrupted, her voice dripping with disdain. "Did you think *you* could manipulate him into setting me aside so that you could take my place in his bed? What else would you have to offer him? Your family connections? Your political acumen?"

Her words stung and made me flinch, but she showed no signs of backing down.

"Kristabella, please—" I tried, but she silenced me with a glare.

"Tell me, Lyra, how long have you been plotting this little scheme of yours?" Her anger seemed to radiate off her, filling the room with an oppressive heat.

"Since before we met," I admitted, shame burning through me. "But you have to believe me— Everything between us— My feelings for you are real."

"Your *feelings*?" Kristabella scoffed, her eyes narrowing. "Do you think I'm a fool, Lyra? How could I ever trust you?"

I stared into Kristabella's eyes, searching for any sign of the warmth and kindness I had come to adore. But all I saw was ice-cold fury, her beautiful gray eyes stormy with betrayal.

She had demanded honesty, so I would give it to her.

I had no other choice.

"Kristabella... you're right," I choked out, my voice barely a whisper. "My... plan was to capture General Thorne's attention— But meeting you changed everything."

My heart raced, and I took a deep breath, steeling myself for what I was about to say.

"Ever since we were first introduced, I've been fighting these feelings growing inside me—this... What I'm feeling—it's a love that I never expected to feel for anyone." I swallowed hard, my throat dry from nerves. "But I can no longer deny it. I am in love with you, Kristabella."

I fell to my knees before her as tears streamed down my face. "Please believe me. I know I don't deserve your forgiveness—but I would do anything to earn your trust again."

Kristabella studied me for a moment, her expression unreadable. Then she spoke, her voice cold and steady. "If you truly wish to prove your loyalty, Lyra—"

"Anything," I gasped.

Kristabella's eyebrow rose. "Help me kill General Thorne."

"Kill the General?" I choked out. My blood was like ice in my veins.

"It's the only way we can truly be together," she continued. "If he dies after our wedding, I will retain his power and position."

My heart thundered in my chest as I considered her proposal. The thought of taking a life, especially that of someone as powerful as General Thorne, terrified me. But the alternative–losing Kristabella–was unbearable.

"Alright," I whispered, my voice shaking. "I'll do it."

"Good," Kristabella replied, her eyes hardening with determination.

As we began to plot the General's demise, my mind raced with conflicting emotions: fear of what we were about to do, guilt for betraying him, and a deep, unwavering love for Kristabella that drove me to such desperate measures.

She reached down and grabbed hold of my arms. She pulled me to my feet and my breath caught as her lips crashed against mine with a desperate passion that took my breath away.

Kristabella's hands roamed my body, expertly undoing the laces of my gown until it fell to the floor in a pool of silk. She guided me to the bed, her touch both gentle and possessive as she stripped away the last of my garments.

"Tonight, my love, I shall take you to heights you've never imagined," she murmured into my ear, her breath hot against my skin. I shivered in anticipation, but also felt a wave of confusion and distress wash over me as I realized the weight of what I'd agreed to.

I lay back on the sheets, fully exposed to her gaze, my vulnerability laid bare before her. Kristabella's eyes devoured every inch of me, and she began to explore my body with her hands and mouth, her skilled touch igniting a fire within me that only she could quench.

"Please, Kristabella," I whimpered, my voice thick with desire. "Take me."

"Your wish is my command," she purred, positioning herself above me. Her strong thighs straddled my hips, her wet heat pressed against mine, eliciting a gasp of pleasure from my lips. She took charge then, rocking forward and back as our mutual arousal lubricated her motions.

I lifted my hips up and gasped at the increased pressure on my clit. Kristabella groaned and her movements became more frantic.

My world narrowed to the sensation of her body against mine, the slick warmth and of her sent jolts of pleasure through me. I moaned and gripped her hips as she rode me with a fervor that left me breathless.

"Submit to me, Lyra," Kristabella commanded, her voice laced with lustful authority. She reached down to wrap her hand around my throat, restricting my breathing and driving my pleasure higher.

"You're mine."

"Yours," I hissed.

I gave myself wholly to her, surrendering my body and soul to the woman who held my heart captive.

As our passion reached its crescendo, I could no longer hold back the storm of emotions that threatened to consume me. Tears streamed down my cheeks, mingling with the sweat and desire that covered our entwined bodies, Kristabella released her grip on my throat and kissed me hard as my orgasm crashed over me. I cried out against her mouth as my body shuddered.

She fell down beside me, breathing hard as she slid her hand between my thighs to drag her fingers through my slick folds.

"Kristabella... I love you," I whispered between ragged breaths, my voice hoarse from the intensity of our coupling.

"Then prove it, my darling," she replied, her gaze locked on mine, daring me to fulfill the dark promise we'd made together. She pulled her hand from my soaking pussy and pushed her fingers into my mouth so I could taste the mingling of our arousal. I sucked on her fingers eagerly until she pulled them back.

"Promise me again," she hissed.

"I'll do it," I said as she leaned forward and pressed her lips against my breasts. She suckled my nipple hard, teasing me with the sharpness of her teeth. "I'll do it," I repeated. "Whatever you want. I just want to be with you."

Her smile was smooth and languid and relief coursed through me as she brushed her fingertips along my jaw.

But what I had agreed to weighed heavily on me even as Krista-bella pressed her lips against mine and I lost myself in her kiss.

Seven

Tension filled the air, thick and palpable as I stood in Kristabella's chambers, trying to make sense of everything that had happened. The weight of my mother's expectations and the promises I had made threatened to suffocate me.

My heart raced with a mixture of fear and anticipation as I considered the path I was about to walk.

Was it too late to turn back?

"Tell me what you want," General Thorne Valerius demanded, his voice low and commanding. His intense, dark eyes locked onto mine. "And don't hold anything back."

Before I could respond, he pressed me against the cold stone wall and pinned my wrists above my head. His lips found mine, and our tongues tangled together in a passionate dance that left me breathless. I could feel the heat of his body through the thin layers of our clothes, and a shiver ran down my spine as he nipped at my lower lip.

"Fuck me, Thorne," I whispered boldly into his ear, feeling an intoxicating mix of power and vulnerability. I looked across the room to where Kristabella stood, her gray eyes wide with desire. "And make sure Kristabella sees every moment of it."

A slow smile spread over her face as she leaned against the doorframe and watched us intently as if we were putting on a show just for her.

Thorne turned to look over his shoulder before he turned back to me, his gaze burning with lust. He took hold of my bodice and held it tight as he pulled a knife from the sheath at his hip.

I bit my lip as he dragged the tip of the blade lightly down my collarbone and sliced through the thin material of my gown. His smile was cold as he tore my gown, leaving me exposed and vulnerable before both him and Kristabella.

My cheeks flushed with excitement, but I held my gaze steady, not willing to give in to my embarrassment.

"Look at her, Lyra," Thorne commanded, his hand gripping my hair tightly as he forced my head to turn towards Kristabella. "This is what you wanted, isn't it?"

"Yes," I hissed, my body trembling with anticipation as Thorne's other hand roamed over my naked flesh. He pinched and kneaded my breasts, causing me to moan softly at the delicious pain.

"Such a beautiful sight," Kristabella murmured from her position in the doorway. The desire in her voice sent shivers through me, and I realized that not only did I crave the touch of the powerful general but also that of the elegant woman watching us.

"Please," I begged, unable to contain the need that surged through me. "Fuck me."

Thorne wasted no time in fulfilling my request. He took hold of my waist and lifted me up, bracing my back against the rough stones of the wall as I grabbed for his shoulders and wrapped my legs around his waist.

He fumbled briefly with his breeches and I moaned as I felt the press of the thick head of his cock against my entrance.

"Take him, Lyra," Kristabella said. "Watch me while he fucks you."

Thorne entered me with one swift thrust, causing me to cry out in a mixture of pleasure and pain. My nails dug into his muscular shoulders as he pounded into me, each thrust pushing me closer to the edge of bliss, but I kept my gaze locked on Kristabella's cold pale eyes.

My head spun with a potent mix of lust and desire as I watched Kristabella slide her fingers between her thighs to rub against her clit.

"Tell me how much you like it," she demanded.

"He— He's so big," I gasped as I reached for her.

She walked forward slowly, her hips swaying seductively as she approached us. "Does he feel better than I do? Does his cock feel better than my tongue?"

Thorne's laugh was low as his fingers dug into my thighs and Kristabella leaned in to press her lips against my throat.

Thorne's pace quickened, and I arched my back so Kristabella could nip at my breasts. I pulled one hand from Thorne's shoulder so that I could tangle my fingers in her long hair and pulled her closer, moaning softly as she kissed the curve of my neck.

Kristabella's teeth grazed the side of my neck and I moaned as her hand slid down between my breasts and down my stomach. My breath hissed through my teeth as her fingers found my clit. She glanced at Thorne and the General's fingers bit into my hips as he fucked me with renewed intensity.

I moaned at the mingling of pleasure and pain caused by his relentless possession of me even as Kristabella's soft lips found mine like an insatiable predator seeking fresh blood.

Her fingers worked my clit, heightening the intensity of the climax that was building inside me.

"Your ecstasy belongs to me," Kristabella whispered. Her eyes burned into mine.

"*I* belong to you," I groaned.

Thorne's cock throbbed inside me, sending waves of pleasure rolling through my body and I cried out against Kristabella's mouth as my orgasm took hold.

I forgot the feel of Thorne's hands on my body as my consciousness shattered into a thousand pieces.

All I could see was her.

~

As I walked away from Kristabella's chamber, my body still tingling and pulsing with the remnants of pleasure, I couldn't help but feel a sense of unease. Despite the incredible passion I had just experienced, the dark cloud of my promise lingered in the back of my mind—

It also didn't help that I had been going my best to avoid my mother and her ambitions.

As I wandered through the corridors, I stumbled upon a secluded garden that I hadn't seen before... I stepped out of the stone corridor and sighed as my feet touched the grass. I slipped my shoes from my feet and tilted my face up toward the crescent moon.

The silvered light was comforting, and I touched the leaves of the night-blooming flowers gently as I walked through the enclosed space.

I eased myself down to the ground and leaned against the stone wall to look up at the stars.

"Can you believe how quickly that Batherst woman has risen in the court?" A woman's voice floated through the night air and I pressed myself against the wall and I held my breath as the voices moved closer.

"Their family should have been forgotten along with the rest," a second woman said. Her voice dripped with disdain and I shivered as I tried to push myself further into the roses.

"You know I agree with you," the first replied. "Have you heard the rumors? She was involved with Lord Palimenteri... some say it's the reason her husband was murdered."

I pressed my hand against my mouth to keep from gasping.

My father—murdered? But—

"I've heard all the rumors," the second woman said with disdain. "It ended quite badly, and there are some who say she's out for revenge—she didn't get what she wanted after she killed her husband."

The first woman laughed. "Indeed, could you imagine Lord Palimenteri choosing such a woman to be anything more than his whore? Impossible!"

My heart seized in my chest as the women laughed, and my throat was tight. My whole body trembled as I pressed myself against the cold, stone wall. Could my mother truly be so vengeful?

The weight of this revelation hit me like a rockfall, and I felt as if the air had been sucked out of my lungs.

I had to confront my mother—her relentless pursuit of Kristabella's destruction had nothing to do with her... But with her father.

I had been manipulated by my own desires...

On my hands and knees I crawled through the dark garden, desperate to flee without being seen.

"That Batherst girl is just like her mother," the second woman said. "She and Lady Palimenteri have been inseparable since the announcement of her engagement to the General."

"The wedding should put a stop to any scheming that might be going on in the shadows," the first woman said. I could hear the smile in her voice and my heart burned with renewed fear—what if she was right? What if the marriage meant the end of my relationship with Kristabella and the General sent me away—what if Kristabella changed her mind?

Blood tears stung my eyes, blurred my vision, and wet my cheeks as I crawled through the grass. I had to escape their scorn.

Their gossip. Every word was like a dagger in my heart and I couldn't bear it.

Finally my hand scraped against stone and I bit back a sob of relief as I scrambled to my feet and slipped into the corridor. I pressed myself against the stone wall as the women moved through the garden and resisted the urge to peer around the edge of the wall to see who they were—my mother would want to know who was talking about us... But I couldn't bear knowing.

I wiped at my cheeks with the long sleeves of my gown and hoped that I had removed all trace of my tears. My mother hated it when I cried.

Weakness.

There was no room for weakness when it came to our plans.

But I was weak.

My love for Kristabella had usurped all of my other ambitions... But I couldn't tell my mother that. I was afraid to admit it to myself.

As I hurried through the stone corridors of the fortress, my mind raced with thoughts of betrayal and the potential consequences of my actions. My muscles tensed, and my heart pounded wildly in my chest as I rushed through the great gates for the fortress and stumbled through the streets that led to my mother's house.

"Mother," I demanded as I burst through the door with a mixture of fear and anger coursing through me. "You need to tell me what is behind your plans... now!"

My mother looked up from her embroidery, her piercing blue eyes narrowing as she took in my disheveled appearance and flushed cheeks. She said nothing for a moment, allowing the silence to stretch out between us like a taut string ready to snap.

"What are you talking about?"

I took a gulp of air and tried to calm my furiously beating heart. "You— I heard rumors—"

"Whatever you may have heard, Lyra, is irrelevant," she cut me off coldly, her voice devoid of any affection or concern. "You would do well to remember your place and focus on maintaining our family's status at court."

"Maintaining our family's status?" I spat, unable to control the fury that bubbled within me. "By helping you to take revenge on one of the most powerful families at court? And what about my father— You said he left us—"

"Enough!" my mother hissed as she slammed her embroidery hoop down onto the table. "You are a foolish girl who knows nothing of the world and its harsh realities. Do not *presume* to judge me or question my actions."

As her words cut through me like shards of glass, I knew that I could no longer stand idly by while my mother wreaked havoc on the lives of those I cared for. I straightened my spine and stared her down, determined to protect Kristabella, the General, and myself from her twisted machinations.

My hands tightened into fists at my sides. "Answer me, Mother! Is it true? Are you really planning on ruining our lives just because of some ancient grudge?"

"Of course, it's true," she hissed, her eyes narrowed into slits. "Lord Palimenteri ruined my life, and now it's my turn to ruin his. And what better way than to use his precious daughter to achieve it?"

I recoiled at her venomous words, feeling as if I'd been slapped across the face. How could this woman be my mother? The same woman who had once held me in her arms and whispered sweet lullabies into my ear?

"Is your thirst for vengeance so strong that you would sacrifice your own daughter's happiness?" I asked, tears welling in my eyes.

"Your happiness means nothing compared to the satisfaction I will feel when I crush those who have wronged me," she snarled. "It's time you learned your place, Lyra. And when *you* are the one the General chooses for his bride, we can begin—"

"Begin—"

My chest tightened, and it felt like the room was closing in on me. I tried to make sense of her twisted logic, struggling to understand how a mother could be so callous towards her own child. But all I felt was an overwhelming sense of betrayal and confusion.

I stood there, trembling with anger and fear, as I stared into the cold, unfeeling eyes of my own mother. My heart pounded in my chest, but I couldn't let her see how truly terrified I was.

"Is that I am to you?" I spat, clenching my fists at my side.

"Sweet, naive Lyra," she cooed, her tone dripping with condescension. "You don't understand the depths of my pain or the lengths I'm willing to go to avenge those who wronged me. Nothing else matters."

"How can you be so heartless?"

"Love is a luxury I cannot afford," my mother replied, her voice colder than ice. "Not when there's vengeance to be had."

"And what if I say no," I retorted.

My mother's mouth twisted. "You love her, don't you? Love is a weakness, Lyra," she said dismissively. "And it will be your downfall if you're not careful. Do you really think that Lady Kristabella Palimenteri cares for you at all?"

"I—"

My heart lurched in my chest. Kristabella had promised me everything—but she had also asked me to murder the object of my first lust... the man who was going to be her husband...

"That's what I thought," she said. Her bitterness hung heavily in the room as she stood. "Tell me, Lyra," my mother began, her voice dripping with malice as she glided towards me, "how far are you willing to go to protect your precious Kristabella?"

I clenched my fists at my sides, refusing to let her see the fear that threatened to overtake me. "Farther than you can imagine."

"Is that so?" she asked, her eyes narrowing menacingly. Her cold hand reached out and wrapped around my throat, forcing me to meet her gaze. My heart raced in my chest, but I stood my ground against her chilling touch. "You do realize that if you defy me, I will ensure that both of you suffer immensely."

"Your threats don't scare me," I spat, though my breath hitched in my throat. A flicker of doubt danced across her eyes, and I seized the opportunity to wrench myself free from her grasp.

My mother sneered at me, her cold blue eyes narrowing. "You think you're so clever, don't you, Lyra? But you would be nothing without me. It isn't your pretty face that has brought you this far—"

"You can't use me for your revenge," I choked out.

"Of course I can," she replied coolly, unfazed by my outrage. "I already have. Your connection to the General and Kristabella makes you the perfect instrument for my ascent. Do you think I won't use this to my advantage? I can reveal your little tryst... I'm sure the High Council will be very interested in this little... intrigue. Don't you agree?"

"Destroying us won't bring you satisfaction, Mother," I said, struggling to hold back my tears as I backed away from her.

"Enough!" she barked, her face contorted with fury. "You'll learn your place soon enough. Now, out of my sight!"

With vision blurred by tears, I ran back toward the fortress. Kristabella was my only comfort—but even she would betray me if I didn't do what she asked. How could I ever find the happiness I sought if this was how my life was to be?

Manipulated.

Used.

And then cast aside when I didn't comply.

Perhaps this was all I deserved.

I stopped running and my heart slammed against my chest in a painful rhythm. I leaned against the cold black stones of the fortress gate and gasped for air as the weight of my own misery crashed over me.

My pursuit of the General had been selfish—my relationship with Kristabella had begun as a manipulation...

I didn't deserve happiness, and I certainly didn't deserve Krista-bella's love and protection. But she was all I had—I couldn't trust my mother and I didn't know how long it would be before she decided to turn against me.

I bit down hard on my lip and tasted blood.

I had to make a decision.

Eight

The moonlight cast eerie shadows across the room, and my heart raced as I grasped the cold silver dagger in my shaking hand. It was the weapon that would change our lives... the fulfillment of my promise to Kristabella.

The plans.

The manipulations.

My own ambitions.

All of it weighed so heavily on me, like an anchor pulling me into the depths of despair.

I traced my fingers over the intricate carving on the hilt of the knife and watched the slender shaft of moonlight as it gleamed off the blade.

"Kristabella," I whispered, my voice wavering with uncertainty. "Are you sure about this?"

"Of course I am, Lyra." Her gray eyes were steely and unwavering, her jaw set in determination. "This is what must be done."

I knew she no longer trusted me as she once had, and I couldn't blame her. My actions had driven a wedge between us, one that seemingly grew larger with each passing day.

"This is for both of us," she said. "But I need to know that you would choose me first. I need to know that you wouldn't betray me if he asked you to."

"Kristabella, I wouldn't—" I protested, tears pricking at the corners of my eyes. "You know I would never hurt you."

"But you wanted to hurt me, didn't you?"

Her gaze was cold and accusing, and it cut me to the core like the sharp edge of the knife I held in my hand. I looked down at the stone floor... anywhere but at her.

"Actions speak louder than words, Lyra. And your actions have shown where your true loyalties lie."

As we stood there, the tension between us was so palpable it felt like a physical force. Whatever happened, we wouldn't be the same after this...

"Fine," I said, my voice barely audible as I fought to keep my emotions in check. "We'll go through with your plan. But know this, Kristabella: I'm doing this for you."

She reached out and took hold of my chin. Her grip "One false move, and we both pay the price," she said.

"The wedding— don't you want to wait until everything is sealed?"

I was desperate for any excuse to delay this task.

Kristabella's pale eyes narrowed. "Everything is sealed," she hissed. "My father has seen to it all behind my back. The wedding is just a formality. My father has given the General permission to do what he wishes with me, which is the only reason I haven't dismissed you from my sight. He wants you."

My mouth was dry and the knife was heavy in my hands.

"But—"

"Do this for me," she said. She gripped my hand tightly and the intricate carving on the handle of the knife bit into my palm with painful pressure that was enough to make me wince. "Free me from this union and regain my trust."

"I will," I gasped.

She kissed me hard, but there was no passion in it and when she released her hold on me and stepped away, I felt... worthless.

"Tonight," she said.

I nodded weakly. "Tonight."

The candles that Kristabella and I had lit bathed her chamber in a dim crimson glow that seemed to pulse in time with the beating of my heart. I couldn't help but feel like a puppet on strings as I watched Kristabella as she lay upon the wide expanse of her bed.

General Thorne stalked the room like a predator, waiting for Kristabella to give the command that we were all waiting for.

The plan was in motion, yet my mind screamed at me to stop, to find another way.

"Come, Lyra," Kristabella purred as she extended her hand to me, her gray eyes dark with desire.

Tentatively, I stepped forward, my body trembling with a mix of fear and longing. I knelt on the edge of the bed and she rose up to meet me.

Kristabella's touch ignited a familiar fire within me, the same one that threatened to consume me.

My lips met hers hungrily and our tongues danced together in a sensual rhythm as her hands gripped my waist in a tight and possessive grip. But my thoughts were clouded by the knowledge of what was to come, and I struggled to push them aside.

But another hand stroked down my spine. "Relax, Lyra," Thorne whispered into my ear. His warm breath sent shivers down my spine. "Give yourself to us."

I moaned as Kristabella pushed her fingers between my thighs and rubbed against my clit as the thick head of the General's cock nudged against my slick entrance.

I wanted them both.

I never wanted this agonizing ecstasy to end and so I allowed myself to be swept away by the tide of lust and pleasure that engulfed us all. Our bodies moved together, lost in a sea of tangled limbs and gasping breaths. I tasted Kristabella's full lips, her fingers teasing and taunting me as she knew precisely how to do. The General's strong hands roamed my body, leaving goosebumps in their wake as he claimed me in ways no one else ever had.

Sweat glistened on our skin as the night wore on, our moans and cries filling the air with an intoxicating symphony. It felt carnal and raw, a primal need driving us to lose ourselves in each other completely. But beneath it all, the fear still lingered, a dark shadow that threatened to swallow me whole.

"Forgive me," I whispered into Kristabella's ear as our bodies pressed together. Her gray eyes met mine, a flicker of confusion and something else–doubt?–danced in their depths. But she said nothing, only pulled me closer, her lips finding mine once more.

As the night wore on, my mind continued to race, torn between the pleasure of the moment and the knowledge of what had to come. The plan weighed heavily on my conscience, our impending betrayal casting a pall over the passion we shared. Yet I couldn't bring myself to stop; the pull of desire was too strong, the seductive allure of their bodies impossible to resist.

And so, as dawn approached and our cries of ecstasy faded into the darkness, I lay there, tangled in the sheets and the arms of General Thorne with Kristabella pressed against my back. My heart pounded with guilt and fear, but I couldn't tear myself away from the warmth of their embrace. I knew that in a few short hours, everything would change, and the thought left me breathless with terror.

"Are you ready?" Kristabella's voice was barely audible as she traced the curve of my spine with her fingers. "Once we do this, there's no turning back."

"I know," I whispered, my voice strained with emotion. "But I can't help but feel like we're making a terrible mistake. Isn't there another way?"

She was silent for a moment and her nails scraped against my skin and made me shiver. "Are you breaking your promise to me? Will you betray me again?"

I turned over carefully, hoping that the General wouldn't wake, and looked into her gray eyes.

"I won't."

I couldn't help but feel that we were all lost, each of us prisoners to our own desires and demons.

My heart ached with the weight of what Kristabella was asking me to do.

The General's deep, rhythmic breaths filled the room and Kristabella grabbed hold of my hand and pushed it under her pillow. I bit back a gasp as my fingers touched the sharp edge of the silver dagger. I couldn't help but feel an overwhelming sense of dread.

"Remember, Lyra," she whispered, her voice both seductive and menacing. "You promised."

I looked down at the sleeping form of the man I had come to admire and desire, his strong jaw slackened in slumber, his dark hair tousled from our passionate encounter. I could still feel the heat of his touch on my skin, the intensity in his eyes when he gazed into mine. The thought of ending his life sent a shudder down my spine.

"Kristabella," I breathed, searching for the words to make her understand. "I have to tell you something... My mother— She is the one who has been using me to destroy your marriage... She wants revenge and power, and she's using me to get it. Your father — It's all to punish him—"

Kristabella's eyes narrowed.

"Please," I whispered, desperation clawing at my throat. "There must be another way."

"Enough!" she hissed, fury etched on her beautiful face. "You are weak, Lyra. And your weakness will be your downfall."

Tears streaming down my cheeks, I shook my head, unable to

accept the path she wanted me to take. "I can't do it," I choked out. "I won't."

"Then you leave me no choice," Kristabella said coldly, her disappointment like a dagger in my chest. "You are banished from my service, and from this fortress. Get out of my sight."

Her harsh words cut through me, leaving me hollow and broken. I had lost everything—my love, my loyalty, and now, my place at Kristabella's side.

"Goodbye, Lyra," she whispered, her voice void of emotion. She pushed me from the bed and I stumbled as my feet touched the cold stone floor. The sun had risen, and I gritted my teeth to know that I would have to find my way back to my mother's house.

There was nothing left for me here.

Abandoned and heartbroken, I staggered through the fortress' stone corridors, abandoned except for a few guards, armored against the assault of the sunlight that crept through the cracks in the stone walls.

I winced as a shaft of sunlight seared my arm, but I didn't cry out.

I had lost everything.

With a cloak over my head, I walked out of the fortress gates and into the city, staying in the shadows as much as I could and bearing the burning heat of the sun that bore down on me.

My heart ached with the unbearable weight of loss, the cold emptiness where Kristabella's warmth and trust once resided, now a constant reminder of my banishment.

I stumbled into the house, my face wet with tears that were already drying in the warmth of the day. I was desperate for something to drink, desperate for a comforting word, anything.

I fell to the floor in the entryway and lay with my cheek against the cold stones, the door open behind me. A shaft of sunlight scorched my toes, but I couldn't find the will to pull them into the shadows.

"What are you doing here?"

My mother's voice was cold and hard.

Her presence only amplified my anguish, but I knew there was no escaping her.

"Kristabella has cast me aside," I whispered, my voice cracking under the strain of my emotions. "And it's all because of you."

My mother snorted and stepped over me. She pushed my feet out of the way with the side of her boot and closed the door.

"Is it? Really?"

I couldn't answer her. "If you hadn't come to my chambers—Kristabella overheard your plotting—she blamed me."

"This began as your plot, dear daughter—or have you forgotten?" my mother hissed.

I pressed my face against the stone and squeezed my eyes shut so I didn't have to look at her. She was right.

"Why did she cast you out?"

"I— I broke a promise."

"A promise," she snorted. "What promise could you have broken?"

"I—"

"Spit it out, girl!"

"She wanted me to murder the General," I choked out. The tears came again, stinging my eyes and pooling on the stones. Drops of pure blood. I was so tired. So tired of all of this.

My mother was silent, but only for a moment. "Ah, my dear Lyra," she sneered as she circled me like a predator stalking its prey. "You're still so naïve. Can't you see? Kristabella never truly cared for you. No one who loved you would ask you to do such a thing. She was merely using you. And now that she's done with you, she's cast you aside like yesterday's garbage."

"Be quiet," I muttered against the flagstones. I didn't have the energy to argue with her. Every inch of my body ached, and every beat of my heart felt like sliding through shattered glass. "I know you're happy to see me like this."

"Perhaps I am," she conceded. The cruelty in her voice made me flinch. "But now, Lyra, you have placed yourself in an even better position."

"What are you talking about?"

"Don't you see it? Now you have the chance to take revenge on both the General *and* that insipid little harlot."

I pushed myself up and looked at her incredulously. "Revenge?! How could you even suggest such a thing?"

"Listen to me, Lyra," she hissed as she leaned down. She took hold of my arm and hauled me to my feet. "I didn't raise you to be defeated this easily. Together, we can bring them both down. We can expose their debauchery to the entire kingdom. They used you. *Abused* you. Kristabella tried to force you to murder the General. She won't be forgiven for such a reason. They will all be ruined, and *we* will rise in their place."

I stared at her, appalled by the depths of her scheming and callousness. How could this woman, who had given birth to me and raised me, be so consumed by her thirst for power and social status that she would encourage her own daughter to seek revenge?

"Mother," I whispered, trembling with the weight of my decision. "I cannot do as you ask."

"Then you are a fool!" she snarled as she released her grip on my arm. I stumbled away from her and only barely caught myself on the doorframe. "You will never achieve greatness if you continue to cling to your misguided morals."

"Perhaps not," I admitted, my voice steady despite the tears that threatened to fall. "But at least I will be able to look at myself in the mirror without shame or regret."

My mother's mouth twisted into a cruel smile. "You say that now, but you will see the wisdom in my plans—and I will be here when you do."

"Leave me be," I muttered. I stumbled toward the stairs and half-crawled to my chambers where I fell onto my bed, not caring that the curtains were half open to let the daylight in. If it burned me to death in my sleep, perhaps I deserved it.

I was too miserable and empty to care.

Several days had passed since my confrontation with my mother, and I could feel her growing restless. Kristabella and Thorne's wedding night was approaching with a speed I didn't want to think about, and I knew that my mother had wasted no time in her scheming, undoubtedly seeking a way to twist this new situation to her advantage.

"Darling, I have found the perfect opportunity for us to elevate our family's standing," she announced one evening, her voice dripping with false sweetness as she entered my chamber.

"I already told you I won't be a part of your schemes," I replied, trying to remain composed despite the fury boiling inside me.

"Ah, but this is different," she said, a wicked gleam in her eyes. "You need do nothing—only accompany me to the fortress. I will do everything, you need only be present and respond as I tell you to."

I narrowed my eyes at my mother. "I'm not going. You won't use me for this—"

"From what I have heard from the gossips in the court, Kristabella Palimenteri has no intention of consummating her marriage to the General. You can confirm this, can you not?"

I shifted uncomfortably.

It was true.

"You don't need to say anything, Lyra. I can see in your face that it's true. Was that your role in all of this? You were to be the buffer between Kristabella and the General? He could slake his lust on you and leave Lady Palimenteri to her own devices... This is what I need to finally expose Lord Palimenteri for the grasping, power hungry man he is... and we can finally claim our rightful place among Evermore's elite."

The irony of my mother's words struck me like a painful blow.

She was the grasping, power hungry monster... but she would never listen to me.

The thought of betraying those I once held dear sickened me, but I knew I couldn't simply allow my mother to continue her malicious plotting. I needed to find a way to put an end to her manipulations while protecting those I cared about.

"Very well," I said with a sigh. "But if we are to expose them, we must do so in front of all Evermore's high society. At the grand ball before the wedding."

My mother's eyes widened at my sudden enthusiasm. "Perfect," she purred, clearly pleased by my submission. "No one will be able to ignore our triumph."

I was abandoned while my mother set about her preparations —new gowns, new jewels—beautiful luxurious things we couldn't afford, but that my mother was determined to have.

In her mind, when her plan was set into motion we would have more money and power than we could ever dream of.

With my mother distracted by her own aspirations, I was able to move unnoticed through the house. One night just before dawn I found myself in the room that I had always thought of as my father's study.

The heavy mahogany desk held neat stacks of leather bound ledgers all covered in a thick layer of dust. I ran my finger through the shroud of time that had settled upon the books and coughed at the glittering cloud that my gentle action raised.

As I backed away from the desk, my foot struck the wall and the sound made me pause. I kicked the wall gently and heard the hollow sound again.

I bent and pulled aside the tapestry that covered the wall and held back a sneeze as dust rained down on me.

It was hard to see in the gloom—but it was there. A secret panel, almost hidden.

I bent down and pushed at it and bit down on my lip to keep

from crying out as the panel opened inward and I almost tumbled inside.

I grabbed for the candle I'd brought into the room and set it on the floor beside me as I peered into the darkness. I held my breath as I reached into the dark space and gasped as my fingers brushed over the edge of a metallic object. With gritted teeth I reached farther into the space and pulled the object forward. It scraped over the wooden boards inside the wall and I held my breath as I hoped that my mother wouldn't notice the noise.

Thankfully, there was no sound from the floor below me—she must have left the house—and I let out my breath slowly.

I pulled the candle forward and the flickering light illuminated a metal box with a golden lock. I frowned as I pulled the box out of its hiding place.

"What are you?" I murmured.

I despaired about the lock, but then remembered the knife-like letter opener that lay in the desk drawer. I rose to retrieve it and pushed the door closed before I returned to the box on the floor.

Hesitantly I inserted the tip of the letter opener into the lock, but as a few moments of frustration, I turned to desperate stabbing.

In three blows I had broken the lock and the lid of the box sprang open.

The letter opener clattered to the floor as I beheld the contents of the box.

Letters, brown and stained with age and... something that looked like blood. Letters tied with a black silk ribbon that crumbled and flaked away in my fingers as I tugged on the ends.

I opened them slowly and read the contents of the pages with breathless anticipation.

It was all here.

Everything I needed.

My mother's secret tryst with Kristabella's father... But my father—his name was mentioned only once.

Demetrius won't stand in my way. Nothing will stand in my way.

I swallowed hard as I read those words again.

What had she done?

There was more... But all of the letters were written in my mother's careful, elegant script. Except for one, written in stiff block letters made with purposeful strokes.

Helena Batherst,

Cease your correspondence with Lord Palimenteri at once. Your letters will be returned to you. Unread. You would be wise to avoid contact with his Lordship. This is your only warning.

In service to his Lordship,

~C.

I re-read the letter and cringed at its terse tone. This was why my mother hated the Palimenteri's. Her letters, some of them sealed, others obviously unfolded and then clumsily re-folded, held all of her hopes and schemes. Her lust for Lord Palimenteri and the power that he held.

She had hoped to take a place at his side—and that the child she carried in her belly would be accepted as his. She reminded him of his promises... his many promises.

Me.

I was the child she spoke of in her letters.

I swallowed hard and put the letters into their stack once more and tied them again with the decaying ribbon.

My mother had poured all of her hatred and her desperation into these letters, only to have them thrown back in her face.

I could understand her anger, even sympathize with it.

But what she had done could not be forgiven—my father—what had happened to him?

The letters were cryptic, but chilling. Had she killed him? Or paid someone to have him killed?

Maybe I didn't want to know the truth.

I tucked the metal box back into the wall and pulled the secret panel closed. I had everything I needed to prove that my mother had a motive for her devious actions.

Unforgivable actions.

She was selfish and devious. She didn't care about me. She only cared about her revenge.

I had to stop her.

Nine

On the night of the ball my mother fussed over me in a way that almost made me believe that she loved me. It was as though I was a young girl again when she had delighted in dressing me up and taking me out into the city streets to show me off—but I knew now that she had only done it in the hope of catching the eye of a wealthy gentleman who might want me for a wife or a mistress... She only ever had her own interests at heart.

Not mine.

Never mine.

But I hadn't known any better when I was a girl.

"You look perfect," my mother purred in my ear as she pulled on the laces of my bodice. "Delicious even."

The dark gown had been fitted to my curves and dipped scandalously low across my breasts.

"Mother— Kristabella won't want me to be there," I said. "What if she has us escorted out?"

"She won't have a chance," my mother snapped. She tugged on the laces and I drew a quick breath as she secured the laces. She smiled and the flash of her sharp teeth made me stiffen. She was ruthless. I couldn't forget that. If she knew that I was planning to betray her, there was no telling what would happen.

"Come," she snapped. "The festivities are already underway, we must be quick."

I followed my mother out of the bedroom and down the stairs, my nerves twisted into knots. I had to keep myself composed and stay focused on my plan.

Luckily for us, it seemed as though the whole of Evermore had been invited to this event and we blended easily with the other upper and middle class citizens who were making their way through the streets toward the fortress.

Flowers and garlands adorned the dark stones and the imposing structure resembled a garden wall instead of a formidable fortress. It was beautiful.

As we entered the grand hall, I couldn't help but marvel at the opulence of it all. The crystal chandeliers glittered overhead and flowers bloomed in every corner. It was as though we had stepped into an enchanted garden, but it couldn't hide the dark intentions that lurked beneath the surface.

My mother's hand squeezed my arm tightly and she leaned in close to whisper in my ear. "Remember what I told you," she said, her eyes gleaming with a fierce intensity.

I nodded stiffly, my jaw clenched tight. I knew what she wanted me to do, but I had another plan. I needed to get closer to Kristabella and find a way to warn her about my mother's scheming ways, but would she speak to me? Or would she be angry...

We made our way through the crowds of guests, my mother stopping every few seconds to flirt with someone or exchange a few words with an acquaintance. It made me feel sick to my stomach—how could she be so charming when her thoughts and plans were so dark?

I was almost relieved when we reached the refreshment table and my mother excused herself to fetch a drink.

It gave me a chance to breathe and scan the room for Kristabella's signature red dress.

But as I turned around, I felt a hand on my arm. I spun around, ready to defend myself, but found myself face-to-face with a tall gentleman dressed in a black suit. His darkly handsome features were etched with a hint of a smile as he looked me over, his eyes lingering on my cleavage.

"Lyra Batherst," he said.

"Do I know you?"

He shook his head. "No, but I've heard a great deal about you—"

"I—"

"My wife would very much like to meet you."

I didn't like the glint in his eyes, or the hold he had on my arm.

"May I have the pleasure of your company?" he asked, his voice smooth as honey.

I tried to pull away, but he tightened his grip on my arm. "I'm afraid I can't."

"Can't or won't?" he asked with a raised eyebrow. "I promise you won't regret it."

"I said no," I snapped, pulling my arm free from his grasp.

He chuckled and stepped back, giving me a mock bow. "Unfortunate, but, as you wish. My wife will be very disappointed." he said before he turned and disappeared into the crowd.

I shuddered and forced myself to focus on my mission. I had to find Kristabella and warn her about my mother's plans before it was too late. But where was she? The sea of people made it impossible to spot her.

As I made my way through the crowd, I caught glimpses of familiar faces—high-ranking officials and wealthy merchants that my mother had introduced me to before. People I'd seen in court when I was at Kristabella's side.

And then I saw her—Kristabella. She stood at the edge of the dance floor, her deep crimson dress flowed around her as she watched the guests twirl across the floor. Her face was serene and beautiful and her dark hair cascaded down her back in waves that I longed to drag my fingers through, but her pale eyes held a hint of sadness that tugged at my heartstrings.

I took a deep breath and made my way over to her.

"Kristabella," I said softly, trying to keep my voice steady. "I need to speak with you."

She turned her head and her eyes narrowed as she saw me. "Lyra," she said, her voice cold. "You shouldn't be here."

"I know," I said quickly. "But I had to warn you about my mother—"

"Warn me?" Kristabella interrupted sharply. "About what, exactly?"

"She's planning something," I said urgently. "Something terrible... She means to interrupt the celebration tonight. I don't know what she's going to do, but she wants to stop the wedding."

Kristabella's eyes widened in shock and horror. "How—"

"She's planning to use me against you, and Thorne— I'm sorry, I didn't want this. I—"

Kristabella's lips pressed into a thin line. "I have to speak to my father—"

I hesitated for only a moment. All I wanted was to throw myself into her arms and beg for her forgiveness. But then my mother's voice rang out across the room, drawing everyone's attention to her.

"Ladies and gentlemen!" she exclaimed, her voice ringing out over the chatter and music. "I have an announcement to make!"

The room fell silent as my mother stepped forward, a sly smile on her lips. She was beautiful in the emerald green gown she had chosen to wear. Ethereal and somehow threatening in her untouchable beauty, but there was cruelty in her smile and in the way her eyes glittered as she looked out over the crowd.

"We are here tonight to celebrate the union of two powerful houses," she said and a ripple of polite applause from the guests accompanied her words. "But there is something about this marriage that you do not know— Lyra— Lyra, come here, child."

She extended her hand toward me and I swallowed hard as I made my way toward her.

"My daughter, Lyra," my mother said. "Has been caught in the cruelest tangle of deceit. Deceit orchestrated and encouraged by Kristabella Palimenteri herself."

There was a gasp from the crowd and murmurs as my mother took hold of my hand and pulled me against her side.

"And my poor daughter, the lovesick fool, could not say no to someone so powerful, even when she knew that the plot would stain our family name—and contribute to the corruption of the most precious members of our elite council."

Her blue eyes glittered with triumph and my throat was tight with fear.

"Tell them, Lyra, tell them how you were convinced to betray General Thorne Valerius—"

My mother's words rang through the room like a death knell, and I felt my heart race in panic. How could she do this? How could she betray me like this? I tried to pull away from her grip, but she held me fast, her fingers digging into my arm painfully.

"I was convinced," I began.

"Speak up, Lyra," my mother snapped.

"I was convinced," I said louder, "convinced and encouraged by my mother, Helena Batherst, to ensnare General Thorne Valerius —to damage his relationship with Lady Palimenteri and take her place in their union."

The murmur of conversation in the room rose slightly and I straightened my shoulders.

"Lyra," my mother said warningly, "we talked about this—"

But I would not be deterred. "My mother sought only revenge against Lord Palimenteri for what she believed to be betrayal and ill treatment—" I pulled the letters from my cloak and held them up.

My mother could not hide her gasp of shock as she recognized them.

I wrenched my arm from her grasp and stepped away. "My Lord Palimenteri," I called out. "Can you confirm this?"

Kristabella tugged on the arm of the gentleman beside her, and Lord Palimenteri, his cheeks flushed with embarrassment, inclined his head. "I can confirm that Helena Batherst made every attempt to become my wife until I realized what she had done to gain my attention... I am ashamed of my weakness."

"You murdered my father," I hissed at my mother.

Her eyes were cold as she looked at me. "Lyra—" her voice held a warning, but I didn't care.

"You murdered him so that you would be free to marry Lord Palimenteri and you could force him to claim me as his child. You wanted power, and you would let nothing stand in your way to achieve it," I continued, my voice rising. "I will not be a pawn in your games, Mother. I'm ashamed to admit that I allowed myself to be corrupted by your promises and deluded fantasies..."

The atmosphere in the room was tense as my mother glared at me, her anger palpable. But then she turned on her heel and stormed out of the room, but at a shout from General Thorne, guards stepped into her path.

"You will stand aside," my mother shouted.

"Take her to the cells," Thorne said grimly. "She will face judgment for what she has done. The disappearance of Demetrius Batherst has been a mystery for far too long."

I watched as the guards led my mother out of the room, her head held high despite the guards' firm grip on her arms. And as the realization of what had just happened set in, I felt tears streaming down my face—tears of relief, but also tears of shame. Someone came to take the stack of letters from my hand— evidence of my mother's delusions and manipulations—but I was too overwrought to care.

The whispers among Evermore's high society were deafening,

the air thick with curiosity and disbelief. Their shock at my revelation was palpable as they tried to process the truth about Lady Helena Batherst.

"Is this true?" one woman asked her companion, her voice barely audible above the din.

"Could she really have done such a thing?" another questioned, her eyes wide with horror.

"Banishment seems too lenient," a man muttered darkly. "She deserves far worse."

Kristabella was beside me now, her hand on my shoulder. "Lyra—"

I shrugged away from her hand and bit my lip to keep from crying harder. "I'm sorry," I said, my voice cracking. "For everything."

"It's not your fault," Kristabella said soothingly. "Your mother was a manipulative woman who knew how to get what she wanted."

"I should have known better," I said, shaking my head.

Kristabella pulled me into an embrace, and I clung to her tightly, taking comfort in her warmth and the familiar press of her body against mine.

And then, suddenly, everything shifted. The room around us blurred as Kristabella pressed her lips to mine in a heated kiss that left me gasping for breath.

For a moment, everything else faded away—the crowd, the music, the drama—and all I felt was her against me, her hands in my hair and her lips on mine.

When we finally pulled away from each other, I felt dizzy with emotion.

The General approached us, and my heart leapt in my throat as he laid a hand upon Kristabella's shoulder.

"Are you all right?" he asked.

Kristabella reached out to sweep a tear from my cheek with the pad of her thumb, and my breath caught as she slid her thumb into her mouth to suck my blood tears from it.

"I— I am," I said. "I'm sorry to have ruined your evening— I— I'll—"

"You aren't leaving," he said. Kristabella caught my wrist and held it gently.

"Please," she said. "We want you to be here."

"But— I don't deserve your forgiveness," I choked out. "I've done—"

"Nothing," Kristabella said with a smile. "You've done nothing."

"Kristabella told me of her plan," Thorne said with a quick smile. "Don't flatter yourself in thinking that this is the only time that one of my lovers has planned my death."

"But—"

Kristabella smiled. "Say you'll stay, Lyra," she said. "Please."

"Please," Thorne echoed.

"But the wedding—"

"Is tomorrow," Kristabella finished. "We want you there."

I swallowed hard and accepted the glass of blood-tinged wine that Thorne offered me. My heart was full of confusion, lust, and desperation. They were everything I wanted.

"I— I'll stay."

Ten

As I entered the great hall the following evening, I was filled with both trepidation and an excitement that had settled deep into my bones. Kristabella had sent me a stunning gown made of rich silk and sewn with so many seed pearls that I had stopped trying to count them.

It was too much, but she had insisted. I was forgiven, and after spending a night in her arms, I was content—whatever she decided our relationship would be after her marriage to Thorne, I would be content.

She had forgiven me.

That was all that mattered.

As I walked further into the grand hall, it was impossible not to notice the way General Thorne's eyes locked onto mine. His intense gaze bored into me like a physical touch and sent shivers down my spine. The pull between us was undeniable, but I would have to forget it.

"Lyra, you look breathtaking tonight," he murmured, his voice low and seductive as he approached me.

"Thank you, General." My voice trembled ever so slightly, betraying the effect he had on me.

As we stood there, I couldn't help but think of how desperately I wanted him. The feel of his strong hands on my body, the taste of his lips on mine, the unbridled passion we had shared—those sensations would be nothing but memories that would haunt me for the rest of my days.

Just like Kristabella...

It was almost impossible not to touch him... but I couldn't.

Just as our conversation was reaching its peak, Kristabella approached us gracefully, her heart-shaped face framed by her luscious black hair. Her gray eyes were warm, but there was a hint of something more—a sly smile playing at the corner of her lips.

"Ah, Lyra, the gown fits you perfectly, doesn't it, Thorne?" she said, her voice rich and welcoming.

"It does," he agreed.

"Thank you, Kristabella," I answered, trying to ignore the growing knot in my stomach. What was she planning? And what did it have to do with me?

"May I steal Lyra away from you for a moment?"

I stared at Kristabella in stunned silence.

"Of course, my Lady," Thorne replied, releasing my hand with a lingering touch that sent a jolt through me.

"Come, Lyra," Kristabella said softly, leading me aside.

Our eyes locked for a moment, and I was struck by just how much I wanted her—but more than that, how much I cared for her.

I loved her. I loved them both.

She smiled and wound her arm around my waist as we walked and I dared to hope that something had changed.

"I have a question for you, Lyra," she said.

"You do?"

My heart raced at the implications of her words, but I couldn't deny the desire that coursed through me for both Kristabella and General Thorne.

Kristabella's sly smile hinted at a surprise she had in store for me. I could feel the heat rising to my cheeks, as if she were teasing out some secret desire I had yet to acknowledge.

She leaned in close. "Lyra," Kristabella whispered, "I have carefully considered our situation, and I believe I have found a solution that will satisfy *all* of our desires."

She paused for a moment, letting her words hang in the air like the scent of the roses that adorned the hall. My throat was dry and my heart hammered against my ribs in a painful tattoo.

"It is clear to me that we both care deeply for General Thorne," she continued, her voice sultry and low, "I wish to renew our old arrangement... I propose that you become both my lover and the General's mistress. I trust you implicitly, and I can think of no one better to share my husband with."

My pulse quickened at her words, and I felt a mix of shock and arousal. The idea of being intimate with both Kristabella and General Thorne—two people who commanded my loyalty and love—sent a shiver down my spine, awakening a desire I thought I would only live in my darkest memories.

"Kristabella," I breathed, my voice shaking with emotion. "Are you certain about this? What will your father say?"

"My father can say nothing after I'm married," she replied, her eyes twinkling with mischief. "Besides, it's not as if there haven't been precedents for such arrangements among the high-born."

As she spoke, I couldn't help but envision the three of us entwined together, our bodies slick with sweat and passion, exploring each other in ways we'd never dared before. The thought made my heart pound and my core ache with need, and slowly, the shock began to fade, replaced by a desperate hunger.

"Yes," I whispered, my voice husky with desire. "I accept your proposal."

"Excellent," she purred. Her eyes darkened with a possessive lust that sent a shiver down my spine even as her lips curved into a triumphant smile. "Then let us not waste any more time. The General awaits us."

She pressed her lips to mine in a kiss that was sweet and gentle at first, and then heated, leaving me breathless when she pulled away.

Kristabella smiled as she tucked a stray curl behind my ear. "Tonight, my darling, you will belong to both of us."

I glanced at the General, and from the smile on his face, it seemed that he had heard every word that we had spoken.

"Tonight," I murmured.

Chapter 10 - Epilogue

I barely remembered the wedding—my mind swirled with the promises that Kristabella had made. The entirety of Evermore's elite society was present for the wedding, and I forced myself to sit tall in my seat with my shoulders back as whispers flew around me.

I had been forgiven, absolved, and had already promised to testify against my mother when she was brought before the council. I was protected by Lord Palimenteri, and there was nothing more that my mother could do to harm me, or anyone I loved.

I would have been content with that.

I would have even been content with banishment if it had come to it, but everything was about to change.

As the High Acolyte spoke the final words of the marriage ceremony, the room came alive with a symphony of colors, sounds, and scents that threatened to overwhelm me. The celebrations would continue until dawn, I knew that much—but it was almost too much to bear.

The heavy velvet curtains that hung from the high ceilings created little secluded alcoves for guests to have secret trysts or conversations, and the flickering candlelight cast shadows over the guests' faces and across the rich furnishings that made everything look surreal and dreamlike.

Perhaps I was imagining all of it.

Perhaps I had been dragged to the cells beneath the fortress with my mother and this was all a hallucination created by my fevered brain.

But then Kristabella caught my hand in hers and pulled me toward the grand table where Thorne waited for us.

A chair had been placed between the bride and groom and as I took my seat I had to ignore the surprised glances and shocked whispers that rippled through the room as Kristabella placed a glass of blood-tinged wine in my hand and Thorne pressed his lips against the side of my throat.

My heart raced with excitement and anticipation as I watched Kristabella pour a glass of wine for herself, and then for Thorne. As we each took a sip of the rich, earthy wine, I relished the heat from Thorne's hand on my thigh, and the pressure of Kristabella's fingers interlaced with mine.

The three of us talked and laughed as if we were old friends, but there was an undercurrent of tension that simmered just beneath the surface. The celebrations were just delaying what we wanted.

As though she had heard my thoughts, Kristabella released her hold on my hand and leaned across me to speak to Thorne, and I traced my fingertips down her spine in a sensual movement that made goosebumps rise on her flesh. "How long do we have to stay here," Kristabella hissed.

"Not long," Thorne said. "This is just..." he glanced at me and his hand moved higher on my thigh toward the heated juncture between them. "Just a small distraction. It's not for us."

"No, it isn't," Kristabella muttered as she straightened and slid her hand into mine once more.

Feeling bold, I slid my other hand into Thorne's lap and rubbed my palm against his groin to feel the hard length of his cock beneath his leather breeches.

He glanced at me and I bit down on my lip to keep from laughing at the frustration in his jaw as he gritted his teeth.

"Can we leave yet?" Kristabella asked. She pressed closer to me and I longed to kiss her soft lips and feel her hands on my body.

"Yes, we can," Thorne choked out. He cleared his throat and

stood. "My lords and ladies, if you will forgive us—my bride would like to go to bed."

The guests applauded loudly as Kristabella's cheeks flushed crimson and she rose from the table and pulled me with her.

My legs were unsteady as Thorne and Kristabella thanked their guests and then walked out of the banquet hall and down the corridor toward the new apartments that they had been given in honor of their union.

My heart pounded in my chest as the grand bedchamber door closed behind us, sealing our trio away from the prying eyes and judgmental whispers of the guests.

The room was a masterpiece of opulence, with a four-poster bed draped in dark silk and velvet cushions scattered across plush carpets. A fire crackled in the hearth and cast flickering shadows against the stone walls.

"Are you ready, Lyra?" Kristabella's voice was soft, her gray eyes dark with desire. I nodded, unable to tear my gaze away from her. Thorne stood nearby, his powerful presence filling the room, anticipation etched on his face as he watched us.

Kristabella approached me slowly. Her fingers trailed up my arm and sent shivers down my spine. Her lips met mine in a searing kiss, igniting a wildfire of passion within me. Our mouths opened, tongues dancing together, tasting each other's hunger. Her fangs grazed my lower lip, a tantalizing hint of the pleasure and pain that awaited me.

As we continued our heated embrace, Kristabella's hands roamed over my curves, deftly undoing the laces of my gown. The fabric fell away, leaving me exposed and vulnerable, yet empowered by the desire in her eyes. She guided me to the bed and urged me to lie back as she undressed slowly to reveal her own perfect form.

I watched in rapt fascination as she crawled onto the bed, her body moving like liquid silk. Kristabella pushed my legs apart as she climbed up my body and I gasped as she pressed searing kisses along my tender flesh.

"I've been aching to taste you," she murmured against my skin. "It's been an agony—"

I cried out as her tongue swept through my folds, tentatively at first, and then with a hunger that made my eyes roll back in my head.

Across the room, Thorne had begun to remove his clothes, watching us move together with hunger in his dark gaze.

My breath caught in my throat at the sight of him, and I felt a renewed wave of desire wash over me as I reached for him. He entwined my fingers with his and squeezed gently before he stepped back.

Kristabella lifted her mouth from my throbbing pussy long enough to look at Thorne. "She tastes so good," she moaned.

"Go on," Thorne encouraged her, his voice rough with need. "Claim her."

Kristabella smiled and pressed her thumb against my clit to make me moan before she slid two fingers inside my slick channel.

"Is that what you want?" she asked me. "Do you want to belong to me?"

I gasped aloud as pleasure rippled through me. "Yes," I moaned. "Please... make me yours."

Kristabella moved up my body, her fingers still working furiously to bring me to climax. She kissed me hard, letting me taste my arousal on her lips, before she turned her head to trail her tongue along my throat.

"You're mine," she whispered.

"Yes." The word hissed through my teeth as Kristabella's fangs sank into my throat with a sharp sting that quickly gave way to indescribable pleasure. As she drank from me, her hand didn't stop moving as she fucked me and created a rhythm that sent waves of ecstasy coursing me. The sensation was intoxicating, like nothing I had ever experienced before. I belonged to her, and she to me, in this moment of perfect symbiosis as my climax crashed over me and left me trembling and eager for more.